Meaghan

Meaghan

by

Jerry B. Jenkins

MOODY PRESS

CHICAGO

Library of Congress Cataloging in Publication Data

Jenkins, Jerry B.
Meaghan.

I. Title.
PS3560.E485M4 1983 813'.54 82-14328
ISBN 0-8024-4321-4

2 3 4 5 6 7 Printing/DB/Year 87 86 85 84 83
Printed in the United States of America

To Dallas Lawrence Jenkins,
priority personified

Chapter One

I awoke to thunder and stared at the clock radio. It was almost 2:00 A.M.; Margo and I had been married twelve hours. I reached for her in the darkness, but she was gone.

I propped myself on one elbow and squinted down the hall for a trace of light from the bath or kitchen. Nothing.

I sat on the edge of the bed and pulled back the curtain, waiting for a flash of lightning that would reveal our borrowed four-wheel drive next to the cabin. Yup, still there.

Dragging on my baggy, floor-length terrycloth robe, I padded stiffly down the hallway and into the huge front room. Long couches faced rows of picture windows on three walls, leaving the heart of the room wide open.

I faced the back of the couch where Margo sat watching the Atlantic crash onto the rocks whenever the electric show lit up the scene. As I moved up behind her, she turned just enough to let me know she knew I was there. Her long, brown hair hung over the back of the couch.

I gently laid my hands on her head and let them glide down her beautiful hair to her shoulders. She sat in her long, silky robe, feet tucked up under her. When she looked up at me and smiled, I could see she'd been crying.

I knelt behind the couch and cupped her face in my hand, brushing her tears away.

"No one deserves to be this happy," she whispered finally, reaching back and pulling me close, burying her face in my neck.

"That's worth insomnia and tears?" I said.

"Some romantic you are. C'mere."

I climbed over the back of the couch and held her. "Really?" I said quietly. "That's *it?* You let me think you'd changed your mind already and had ventured out into a storm to leave me, and all the while you're sitting here happy enough to cry?"

"You didn't think I'd gone anywhere, Philip Spence. Where would I go? You're the only thing I want, and anyway, you're everything I've got."

"Ho! Then it's a good thing I'm all you want!"

"That's not what I meant. Oh, you know what I meant."

"Of course I do. I've been thinking the same thing about you. I've never been in love before, you know."

"Is that true?"

"Yes, I'm serious. I thought I was once. Thought so very much. Even up until the time I met you, which was a couple of years after it was over."

"Philip, I really don't think I want to talk about this on my wedding night."

"Yes you do, because it ends well. You're the reason I know I've never been in love before. What I felt for you was so much more than anything I'd ever felt for anyone before, that I knew I'd never actually been in love. You're the standard by which I judge my past."

"Your past relationships, you mean."

"No. Everything. You think I'm making too much of this?"

"Yeah. But I love it. Now shut up and kiss me."

"Don't mind if I do."

Over coffee the next morning, Margo was in the mood for business. "What'd you think about that girl on the plane, the one who took our business cards?"

"The stewardess with the doe eyes? What do you mean, what did I think about her?"

"They don't call them stewardesses anymore, Philip. She's a flight attendant. Do you think she'll call, or was she just being polite?"

"I don't know. I can't imagine she asks everyone for a business card. She lit up when she heard we were private investigators. She just might call."

"I think so, too. She was pretty."

"Yeah, those eyes. Like a doe, like I said. Big, dark, wary, fearful. Sweet."

"She *was* that. What was her name again?"

"Meaghan."

"Right, Meaghan with the *h*."

"She sure was quiet, wasn't she? That's why I think she's got a problem. If there's one thing you learn on a jet plane, it's to talk loud."

We had been in first class the day before, a first for both of us. I hadn't done a lot of flying, probably not even as much as Margo, but I sure noticed the difference in first class. And with TransCoastal Airlines, even the stewardesses, oops, flight attendants, dressed differently in first class.

Meaghan Hanekamp was a small, delicate-appearing girl with perfect, creamy skin, a hint of blush, short, stylish hair, and classy, understated jewelry. At first I thought she was talking softly because she had been trained to do that in first class, for the sake of the executives. We were the only couple there.

But I could hear the other first class attendant talking loudly enough. When Meaghan approached and asked if we wanted champagne or orange juice, I had to lean forward and almost read her lips. She seemed preoccupied.

I asked if she was new. "Oh, no, sir," she said. "You have to have two full years of service before being assigned to first class. I was just assigned, but I'm in my fourth year." She started to move away and then turned back. "And you're newlyweds, aren't you?"

"How could you tell?" Margo asked.

"I don't know what it is," she said, almost shyly. "But I'm never wrong. Honeymooning in Boston?"

"In a cabin on the Atlantic, just outside Boston actually."

"Sounds wonderful. I'd like to get away myself."

Later in the flight, when she had a minute, she leaned on the seat ahead of us and asked how we met. We told her where, but we didn't tell her under what circumstances. Margo doesn't like to be reminded of her difficult past every time someone casually asks how we met.

It was when she heard what we did for a living that she sprang to life. She had been polite, interested, charming, though quiet and still somewhat fearful looking. "We work for a detective agency in Chicago that's in the process of changing leadership," I said, wondering if she had even wanted that much information.

Apparently she did. She suddenly became very animated and began asking all about it. I told her that the owner had recently left to take a state government job and that our new boss would be a former Chicago homicide detective sergeant. For some reason, all the details got her going.

I thought she was fascinated that we worked at the same place in admittedly unusual jobs. "We're the only two regular investigators left," I said. "Wally, that's the new boss, is going to be very involved in the investigations, of course, but past us, there's no one else but a receptionist."

"Do you have business cards?" she asked. We each gave her one. "EH Detective Agency," she read. "What's the EH stand for?"

"Just the initials of the owner, the guy who's leaving. He'll still own it, but this Wally will be running it for him."

"Interesting," she said, and I wondered why she thought so.

"Come by and see us sometime," Margo suggested. "There's not much to see, but if you're that interested in detective work—"

"It's not that so much," Meaghan had said. "It's just that I might need to call you sometime. I'm based in Chicago, but it seems I spend as much time in L.A. and Boston as anywhere."

"Well," Margo said, chuckling, "the welcome mat is out in Chicago, but Boston is one place we don't want any visitors."

We all laughed.

"No one could find us here," Margo said as we finished breakfast and did the dishes. "The only people who know where we are are your parents, right? Right? Philip?"

"I'm sorry, sweetheart," I said. "I was thinking. What was it?"

"I was saying that no one knows where we are except your parents."

"Right. Though I have an idea Wally or Bonnie *think* they know."

"Wally's a detective and a born snoop, but how would Bonnie know?"

"She takes all our calls. Who knows what she knows? She somehow knew we were flying first class."

"Yeah, and *I* didn't even know that until we got on the plane. Why didn't you tell me, Philip?"

"You're hard enough to surprise as it is. Speaking of someone's taking all our calls, you know what I like best about this place? No phones. Don't you love it?"

"Oh, it's great. I'm not sure I'd want to say it's what I like *best* about the place, but it's nice, yeah. I'm a little nervous about what we're supposed to do in case of an emergency, though."

"Are you kidding, m'dear? You happen to be married to Jock Lumberjack!"

Even Margo, nervous about emergencies without a phone, couldn't stifle a giggle about *that* ridiculous claim. I was the one who had nearly killed myself and an associate the first time I had to climb down from a second-story apartment patio on a surveillance detail.

"Oh, Philip, look!" she said, drying her hands and then draping an arm around my waist. "The sun! It's going to be a perfect day for sightseeing!"

"The sun?" I muttered. "Margo, I think the sun comes up *every* morning. Are we gonna celebrate it every day of our married life?"

She jabbed me in the ribs. "What's on the schedule, Jock, or Jack, or whatever it is you call yourself?"

I pulled out the brochures full of landmarks and historical sights, but suddenly the normally refined Margo was mimicking the way I usually talk.

"Oh, I know we're gonna see all that stuff," she said, "and I don't much care in what order. What I want to know is, when and where will we be for dinner tonight? We're talkin' fresh creatures from the deep, Philip, and I'm skipping lunch to be ready!"

For the next four days we exhausted ourselves swimming, sailing, canoeing, walking, getting sunburned, sightseeing, and doing some big league eating neither of us had ever dreamed of before.

Ominous weather reports by midday Thursday sent us to a discount store where we picked up a couple of table games and a puzzle in case we had to stay in Friday. We also stocked up on our favorite foods. It proved a smart move. It drizzled all the next morning, and we got a chance to really relax.

"I'm glad it turned out this way, Philip," Margo said at lunch. "I'd have been dead by tomorrow night if we hadn't gotten this break."

"You lonely for other people?"

"No sir."

"Still miss the phone?"

"Nope."

"Really? That's progress."

"Well, I do miss the security of it a little. Even with you around, Jock."

"That's what I thought."

We were lazily working on the jigsaw puzzle late in the afternoon and trying to work up an appetite for a couple of steaks when the black clouds rolled in and the wind kicked up. Suddenly we were in the middle of a storm that made the Sunday night thundershowers seem like a sprinkle.

"I just love storms, don't you, Philip?"

"Sure."

We dragged the table over by the window, but we had lost interest in the puzzle. Every few minutes the lights dimmed momentarily and Margo jumped. "We'd better find the candles before we need them," she said, heading for the closets.

"I'm glad the oven is gas powered," I said. "It's hard to candle a steak past medium rare."

At six o'clock, Margo put the steaks on, and in the pitch of a raging storm I thought I saw something illuminated by a streetlight several hundred yards below us on the steep winding road that led only up to our cabin.

I stood and stared, moving closer to the window and pressing against the glass. Margo called something out to me from the kitchen, but I wasn't listening.

From where I stood I could see three of the street lights on the narrow, gravel road. And whatever I had seen had passed the first light. The wind blew horizontal sheets of rain past the lightpoles, and I glued my eyes on the second, hoping to get another glimpse. We were probably a half mile from that third light pole, so I had just two more chances to see it or him or whatever before it would come into view at the end of our drive.

I didn't know whether to say anything to Margo or not. Was it an animal? Someone lost or in trouble? The agent who had rented us the place? I decided that if I didn't get a good look under the second light, I'd ask her to watch the third with me. I wanted to judge the speed too, in case we had to prepare in any way.

Margo had said something again, and sensing that I was lost in thought, joined me from the kitchen. "What is it, love?" she said. I half turned to respond when I saw it again, under the second light. I tried to cover and pretend I was just watching the storm, and I almost missed it again. It looked like a person, bent against the wind and driving rain, carrying something and maybe wearing a hat. It seemed to be charging steadily on.

As it moved out of the light once again, I said, "Margo, keep your eye on that third light pole down there. Someone is coming this way, and I'm guessing it will take him a half hour to get here. See if you can make it out. Maybe I'm seeing things."

Margo wiped her hands on a towel and leaned against me, staring out the window. She shivered. "Who could it be, Philip?"

I didn't answer.

"Maybe we should take the four-wheel down and pick him up," she said.

"Margo, we don't even know who it is or what he wants."

"And we don't have our guns."

"They wouldn't have let us on the plane with them. Anyway, we're not licensed to carry weapons in this state."

"There! Look!"

The figure had moved into the edge of the light of the third pole, but as we both peered out, a close bolt of lightning illuminated the woods around our place, produced an instant thunder blast that rattled the windows, and plunged us into darkness.

Even the street lights had gone dark.

Margo groped her way back to the kitchen and located a couple of candles and some matches.

"Wait!" I said. "Don't light 'em yet! If there's no light up here, whoever it is will never make it. In fact, maybe we oughta turn the switches off so when the power does come on, we won't be sitting ducks."

"Sitting ducks for whom, Philip? Why assume this person is after us or means us harm? Whoever it is could be just lost, you know. And with no street lights, what is he supposed to do now? I think we should at least turn the lights on in the four-wheel drive so he knows there's shelter up here."

"You're a more trusting soul than I am, but you're probably right. I s'pose if we can get out and turn the lights on, we could just as easily drive down there and have a look. If it looks like someone we don't want to have anything to do with, we can just drive back."

"I don't know, Philip. It would have to look like the Hunchback of Notre Dame before I'd let myself leave somebody in a storm like this."

"Turn the steaks down, kid."

Without an umbrella, all we could do was shuffle to the car together under the scant protection of my extra coat. The rain was cold, and we fought the wind to close the door. The headlights showed bushes and trees leaning and bending.

I flipped the four-wheel drive switch and started the steep decline from our driveway. "I can't imagine anyone being able to move on this road without light," Margo said. "He's probably huddled under a tree somewhere."

"Maybe it's someone who knows this road and is still moving by staying on the pavement. If he's sitting under a tree at this elevation, he's asking for lightning trouble."

I snaked slowly down the road, riding the brake to avoid surprises. With nothing but headlights and no road markings, I would have had trouble memorizing all the sharp curves even if I'd been a long-time resident.

Margo shivered in her parka and fiddled with the radio, trying to find weather news. When she found it, she wished she hadn't.

"Nearly the entire eastern seaboard is socked in under a storm that could continue until dawn, thunderstorms continuing long into the night with no break in sight."

She turned the radio off and helped me watch the road. It was impossible to get a good view through the flapping wipers as they struggled to keep up with the downpour.

Coming around one long turn we saw city lights in the distance from a cliff and knew our intruder could only be on the left side of the road heading up. We were within about 100 yards of the streetlights we had seen from our windows when a tiny figure appeared before us, waving one arm and trying to keep a grip on a shoulder bag with the other.

Chapter Two

"It's a girl!" Margo said.

It *was* a girl, but I still didn't want to take any chances. I stopped about ten feet in front of her and depressed the high beam button, making her hide her eyes. Fearless and impulsive as ever, Margo leaped out and tore off her parka, throwing it over the girl's head and shoulders and walking her back to the vehicle.

I felt like a fool sitting there dry and safe while they climbed into the front seat. The girl's bag slid down between her feet, and she clutched the parka more tightly around her, using her hands to vigorously rub her hair and dry off her face.

She could hardly speak, she was shuddering so hard. "Oh, thank you!" she managed, just above a whisper, but with a voice low enough to tell us she was no child. "The cabbie wouldn't come up here. Thank you so much!"

Margo put her arm around the girl and held her close, trying to stop her trembling. "What are you doing up here, anyway? Our cabin is the only one left past here."

The girl straightened up and pulled the parka away from her face, trying to get a good look at Margo. I instinctively turned on the inside light, exposing a delicate face under short, plastered-down hair that stuck to her forehead.

"It's you!" she said, louder now. "I found you!"

"Meaghan?" Margo said incredulously, staring at me over the girl in her arms.

"You don't know what I went through to find you! And I know you'll never forgive me for barging in on your honeymoon, but I need help."

Margo found her something to change into, wrapped her in a musty old army blanket, and dried Meaghan's hair, wishing we had power and could use a blow dryer.

I worked around them, setting an extra plate and stabbing the steaks out of the oven.

"I can't believe you saw me from up here. If you hadn't come for me, I don't think I would've made it. It took me three days of calling the people who rent these kinds of places before I found the guy who had rented to you. I didn't even know if you rented under your own name or if he would tell me the truth or what, but I'm afraid I kinda lied about a family emergency, and he didn't want to, but he told me where you were. He tried to tell me how far you were from the main road, but I thought he was just trying to protect you."

"You lied about a family emergency?" Margo repeated.

"In a way, but there *is* a family emergency."

"Someone in your family is in trouble?"

"Yes. I am. I feel terrible about being here like this. I wanted to wait until I knew you were back in Chicago."

"Nonsense," Margo said. "We know no one would interrupt a honeymoon without a good reason, don't we Philip? So forget about that and tell us what's wrong."

Margo had surged ahead, not waiting for my reply. Fortunately.

"First of all, no one at TransCoastal knows where I've been for the last two days, so I'll probably lose my job. That's bad, but it's not as bad as my job has been for the past several months."

"Here," Margo said. "Eat something."

"Not bad," Meaghan said. "From lost in a storm to a steak dinner." And with that she was abruptly in tears. Margo looked at me again, wondering.

We couldn't get her to eat anything, but she insisted that we finish our supper. We saved a plate for her in the fast fading refrigerator and joined her on one of the couches in the living room. With her head wrapped in a towel and her body in the old blanket, she made an eerie, shadowy picture in the candlelight. The setting and the lighting were right for a scary story. And she had one.

"I was transferred to Chicago, because I asked to be, about six months ago. I thought I would like living there, and I wanted the change, new flight routes and new crews and all that.

"But this L.A. to Boston crew was tough to get next to. I'm sorta straight, you know? And that sometimes makes it hard for me to hit it off with people right away. They want to do things I don't want to do and stuff like that."

"Like what?" Margo asked, while I sat wondering if Meaghan was expecting to stay the night.

"Like partying, staying up all night, drinking, running around, things like that."

"Uh-huh. And that's not what you, I mean, that's not your—"

"Right, that's not me, OK? I mean, I like to have fun, but I was raised better than that. I was never smart or good in school or much of a reader or anything, but I was raised to work hard and follow the rules and do what was right.

"But anyway, I couldn't make friends with this new flight crew, so when my problem started, I didn't have anybody to tell."

Finally, we were going to get to her problem. I thought.

"What was I supposed to do, go running back to Mom and Dad? I've got a brother who does that now, mooching off them and running home whenever something goes wrong. I had more pride than that, but it kept getting worse, and I knew I would have to tell someone, but I didn't know who until I met you guys."

She smiled at us and I worked up a reciprocal grin. I wanted to push her to get on with her story, but I had learned from Margo, one of the best and most patient—and most silent—interviewers I had ever seen, that you get more by waiting and listening.

Margo even listened with her body. She leaned forward, knees to her chin, head cocked, keeping eye contact, nodding frequently, and raising her eyebrows.

"Well, I tried to make friends with the regulars, and I think they finally accepted me. They quit asking me to join them at their parties and nightclub hopping and all that, but at least they started being civil. They said please and thank-you when we served meals on the flight and had to work together.

"They even smiled at me when I showed up and said hi and good-bye and asked about my family. There was still some kind of a distance or something there, but I couldn't put my finger on it. In a way I was glad they quit asking me to do stuff with them, but in another way I kinda wish they had at least asked again once in a while. That way I could have told them no without seeming like I thought I was better than them or something. Maybe that had been the problem. Maybe I had turned them down and had given them the idea that I thought I was above them. I still didn't want to go with them. But I wanted to be able to turn them down nicely and thank them for asking and maybe suggest something else we could all do. They might have all thought I was funny or out of it, but who knows? Maybe they would've come with me."

"Come with you where?" Margo said. "Where *do* you like to go and what *do* you like to do?"

"Believe it or not, I'm a sports nut, and I like country music. I have friends who go with me to stuff like that, but I wouldn't have dreamed of asking the people I work with. That wouldn't have been their thing at all. But if they asked me again to one of their parties, I would have asked them. You never know."

"But anyway," I said, unable to hold back any longer, "this problem that you didn't feel you could take to them—"

Margo shot me a glance, wishing I would wait.

"Yeah, well, maybe I could have taken it to them, you know, because we had become so friendly lately. One time when Carole, that's the senior attendant on our crew, was going on her vacation in Michigan, I asked her if she would mind dropping a package off at the Grand Rapids airport for my mother. She was happy to, and I've done the same for her lots of times since, but still we're not close, and I wouldn't tell her personal things."

"Personal things?" Margo said.

"The same man has been on all my flights for the last two months."

She shook as she said it and pulled the blanket more tightly around her. It was as if she had never said it aloud before. My inclination was to make less of it than she did, but I didn't know if that kind of a coincidence was significant or not.

"This is someone who commutes from L.A. to Boston everyday?" Margo tried.

"This is no commuter," Meaghan said, spitting the words out. "This is a nut with a lot of money, and I think he's got a thing for me."

"Why does he have to be a nut?" I asked.

"Because he books his flights under different names—I checked because he's driving me crazy, always showing up, and I mean always. It doesn't matter when or where or how full the flight is, this guy winds up on my flights and in my section, no matter what."

"Why would he check in under different names if he has a thing for you?" Margo asked. "It seems he would want you to know who he was and that he was interested in you."

"He doesn't. He wears disguises most of the time. In fact, since the third or fourth time I saw him, he's tried to hide the fact that he's the same one. He's even dressed up as a woman a few times."

It was all I could do to keep a straight face. "Are you serious?" I said.

"Of course. You think I'd kid about something like this? He's not a big man, and he's tried to fool me with hats, mustaches, beards, different clothes, even nail polish in his woman disguises."

"How can you tell it's him every time?" Margo asked.

"I'm big on hands," she said. "Even without looking again, I can remember that your husband has straight, thin fingers and that he keeps his nails short but doesn't bite them. And you—oh, I'm so sorry I forgot your name—"

"Margo."

"Of course, Margo. It was on your card; I'm sorry. Margo Franklin Spence, right?" Margo nodded. "Anyway, Margo, you have longish nails, but not too long, and you keep them very beautifully done, at least on your last flight you did."

"And you noticed something about this guy's hands?" I asked.

"He has half a nail missing vertically on the pinkie of his left hand. It's looks like just a tiny slit or fold in his nail, hardly noticeable, but he is unable to hide it, even with polish when he's dressed like a woman.

"He never talks to me. The third time I saw him, that was three flights in a row, I said something to him about the fact that he'd flown with us pretty frequently that week, but he denied it. That was the last time I saw him in his regular clothes and looking like himself—until this time. But I'm telling you he's been on every flight since then, both ways, avoiding me and pretending to be someone else each time. But he's always there, always under a different name when I check by seat numbers later, and he's got me spooked."

"Me too," Margo said. "What do you think his game is, and what do you want us to do about him?"

"I think he's crazy. I know he must be rich or be an airline employee or know someone because his flights are expensive, and he knows my schedule. I want you to get him arrested or at least off my back, if I still have a job."

"Have you thought about quitting your job?"

"Over this? You mean run from this? It wouldn't do any good. Did I say I saw this guy *only* on my flights? I saw him, or someone who could pass for him—in the dark I can't get a look at his hands, but I know who it is—in the parking garage in the basement of my apartment building on a day when I called in sick. I called in sick just to avoid him for a day, and I'd swear I saw him.

"I saw him in a car across the street from a boutique in Los Angeles one afternoon between flights. He wore shades and a walrus-type mustache, but it was him."

The lights came on and Margo jumped up to get the hair dryer. "When I get back, I want to know what happened this week, two days ago, that made you leave your job without telling anyone."

Meaghan leaned over and blew out the candles, then stood and moved to the window where she noted that the storm had not died down, even though the power had been restored. She noticed in the reflection that I was watching her and she turned and smiled shyly.

"Do you think I'm crazy?" she asked, surprising me, because I wasn't sure.

"I'm wondering if your stalker is crazy," I said, covering, relieved that Margo had returned.

"Then you think he's stalking me too?"

"No. I don't know. I mean, I shouldn't have said that because I don't know enough yet."

"So tell me about two days ago," Margo said, talking over the noise of the dryer. "What happened?"

Meaghan hid her eyes in her hand, either to protect them from the heat of the dryer or to avoid looking at me when she talked.

"He was on the same flight you were on," she said.

"In first class?" Margo asked.

"Of course. He's always where I am."

"Which one was he?"

"He would've been a couple of rows behind you."

"What was he wearing?"

"A western-type outfit, something new for him."

"You're sure it was him?"

"I'm always sure. He was trying to look older with a big hat and a long gray wig over his ears. But he never remembers to cover those hands. Anyway, we've been back and forth between here and Chicago and L.A. several times since then. I've alternated between first class and coach and the only time I crossed him up was when I traded with Carole just before takeoff. But he was still on the plane.

"I started seeing more of him away from the planes. His cab followed mine to my hotel in Los Angeles. I thought I saw him again near my apartment in Chicago. And then, while he was hanging up a garment bag on the flight here Wednesday morning, I saw he was carrying a gun. We're supposed to report stuff like that, but how could a guy with a gun get on a plane anyway? I didn't want to try to turn him in because I didn't know what kind of a can of worms I'd be opening. He'd had a lot of chances to hijack the plane over the last several weeks, and I was so convinced that he was on those flights because I was on them—for what reason I didn't know—that I certainly wasn't going to aggravate him by getting him in trouble."

"Is it possible he's an employee of the airlines or some government agency involved in security?"

"I wondered about that too, but why disguise yourself and hide from the flight crew? If you're there to protect them, let them know. Anyway, the metal detectors take care of security—at least they're supposed to. But if this guy got on with a gun—"

"Apparently, he was supposed to," Margo said. "You're probably right that he has access to the brass somewhere along the line to always know your schedule and then to be allowed on with a weapon. Strange. You're sure he's not after anyone else?"

"That's crossed my mind, but he's there when I'm there, regardless who's flying the plane and who else is on vacation or taking days off or what. I don't know if he's there when I'm not, because I've never asked. But I did check the flight list one day when I got sick and had to leave the plane before takeoff. I went straight home to bed and called TransCoastal's Chicago ticket office. I asked if any of several people were on board, using all the names I had seen him use in the past. They told me he had been ticketed under one of those names, but that he had canceled out just before takeoff. If you don't think I felt watched that day . . ."

"Unbelievable," Margo said.

"That's what I used to think," Meaghan said. "Until it started happening to me every day."

"And Wednesday morning it got to you because of the gun?" I said.

"Yeah, that and the fact that he was back with no disguise. Maybe he thought I'd never been onto him before and he could start over with his disguises. I don't know. Anyway, I had met you two and I knew I had had enough. I told Carole and Dwayne—he's another attendant—I was sick, and I left in a hurry.

"I was on the phone calling your office when he came running by. I pressed up against the phone as far as I could, praying he wouldn't see me, and somehow he didn't. All I got at your number was an answering service, so I hurried back to the plane and told them I was all right, but just as we were about to take off, we were delayed a moment, the doors were opened, and he returned."

"Did you try to get off the plane again?" Margo asked.

"I couldn't. It was too late. What was I going to do—say I was sick again? It would have looked terrible. I *was* able to get out of first class, which was where he was booked, and that felt good for a while. But then he followed me through the airport in Boston. Before that, I don't think he was ever aware that I knew he was following me. But this time I started running, ducking into washrooms, turning this way and then that way, but he stayed behind me about forty feet. When I slowed, he slowed. Finally I was able to lose him, and that's when I checked into a hotel and started calling all the rental agents in this area to see if I could locate you. It wasn't that there was anything new happening with him this time. But I had seen that gun, and that was enough for me."

Chapter Three

I might have had trouble believing Meaghan Hanekamp's story, had it not been for the sheer lunacy of the idea that someone would make one up like it. Like magic, the blow dryer and a bit of makeup brought back to us the soft-spoken little beauty from the flight to Boston.

What I really wanted to do was to talk with Margo to see what she was thinking. She always had better insight into situations like this one. I frankly wouldn't have minded cutting our honeymoon short one day and jumping into this case with both feet, but I wasn't about to suggest it because I didn't know what Margo would think.

"Do you think your man has followed you here?" I asked.

"I really don't. The problem is, he must have been following me a lot before I finally caught on several weeks ago, and maybe plenty more after I *did* catch on. Something tells me he's good at what he does, and I wonder how many people notice that little fingernail. Without that and a little paranoia, I never would have put it together."

"What are you thinking, Philip?" Margo asked.

"Well, the first thing we have to do is to get Meaghan back on good terms with her employers. What's the worst that can happen to you for not reporting in to work?"

"I could be fired."

"Any way out of it?"

"Lying. I could come up with a real winner."

"But you say you were raised better than that. It's bad enough you had to stretch the truth to find us, but why compound that with another?"

"I know, Margo. It's just that—"

"It's just that we don't want to preach," Margo began earnestly, not harsh. "But I've got to tell you, our agency is built on truth and trust, and we have to know if we can trust you; we have to know whether we can believe every word of your story."

"You can."

"Well, then, maybe now is a good time to start practicing the truth so you won't be tempted to stretch it even a little in your dealings with us. Can we assume you won't?"

"Of course, but how do I get my job back without lying and without telling the whole truth either? You don't want me to tell my supervisor what's been going on, do you?"

I interrupted. "And may we assume that you're engaging our services, the EH Detective Agency, I mean?"

"I don't have a lot of money—"

"You'll need some, not a lot, unless this requires a lot of flying. But we need to know. We need to hear you say it before we can get back to Chicago and solidify it on paper, that you are asking us to handle a case for you."

"That's what I want, yes, but how do I—?"

"Get your job back?" Margo said. "All you can do is try. I think you'd better call whoever you need to call tonight and tell them you had some personal problems, that you have taken a step toward resolving them, that you know you were wrong in leaving your job without telling anyone, and that you're sorry. It won't happen again, and you're appealing on the basis of your good record. If they want to put you on probation or suspend you or whatever, you'll accept it, but you'd like to get back to work immediately, on tomorrow morning's flight to Chicago."

"You make it sound so easy, but even if it works, I don't *want* to go back to work, and the last thing I want to do is be on that flight tomorrow morning. I just know he'll be there, even if he lost me for a couple of days. He has a way of resurfacing. Remember, he hasn't missed a flight of mine for two months. That's a lot of flights."

"We'll be with you," Margo said impulsively, then looked ashen. "I'm sorry, Philip. I know we have to talk about this."

I started to tell her it was all right, but Meaghan jumped in. "Oh, no, no, I just couldn't let you. Absolutely not. I'd never forgive myself, ever. That would be worse than going back by myself."

"What do you say, Philip? It's not that this hasn't been the greatest week of my life, but the weather is apparently not going to break. Working together is better than doing nothing here all day tomorrow."

"I agree," I said, surprising them both. "First we have to get Meaghan back to her hotel—"

"It's just a motel about five miles from here."

"—and get her on the phone to where?"

"I'd have to call Chicago actually."

"Then she can get us on that same flight, we'll pick

her up in the morning, and we'll work out a plan so she can tell us if her man is on the plane and what seat he's in."

"I don't think we should go to the airport with her," Margo said. "I know you're thinking that would protect her from the man with the gun, but let's take the chance that he'll somehow know, as he always has, that she's going to be on that flight. He'll be waiting for her at the airport, and she shouldn't be seen with us."

Meaghan was speechless. She had seen us shift into high gear, from trying to decide whether we were willing to give up the last soggy day of our honeymoon to bouncing strategy off each other.

"Anyway," Margo continued, "your buddy is running us to the airport so he can get the four-wheeler back. Let's not involve any more people in this than necessary."

"All right then, we'll just be sure to be on your flight. Don't act like you know us. Just treat us like any other passengers, OK?"

"All right, Mr. Spence, but you know I won't be able to be in first class, even if they do let me work tomorrow. Anyway, I've got to get my outfit dried before morning."

"Then I'll go with you to a laundromat, Meaghan, and Philip can be switching our reservations to that flight. We'll just downgrade them to coach."

"You can use the phone in my room," Meaghan said.

"No, we'd better not be seen at your motel," Margo said. "After you've made your call and we're done with your outfit, you can take a cab to your motel. Just in case he's watching."

"But what if he's through watching and is ready to kill me when he finds me alone?"

Neither of us spoke for a moment. "I know you're scared," Margo said finally. "And I'd hate to be wrong about this. But nothing you've said leads me to believe that you're in real danger with this guy. Hasn't he had the chance to harm you? He must know where you live."

"Yeah, he does. I don't know, Margo. I'd rather you guys were with me all the way."

"Am I wrong, Philip? Tell me; I can take it."

"I think you're right, babe, but I don't blame Meaghan for being scared. I won't sleep too well tonight myself, knowing he's out there somewhere."

"You could stay with us," Margo tried, but that brought Meaghan to her feet.

"Not a chance!" she said. "No way! Let's get going."

I was glad.

Margo and I sat in the laundromat while Meaghan used the phone for her call to Chicago. She came back trying to hide a smile. "It worked," she said. "Honesty worked, just like Mom—and you, Margo—always said it would. Thanks."

"What'd they say?"

"I get a double pay dock and I'm on probation for six months. Any more incidents, and I'm gone, no questions asked. Not bad, I think, under the circumstances."

Meaghan called a cab, and we decided to wait at the laundromat for her call, telling us everything was all right and that she was in her room and secure before we headed back to our place. While we waited, I called Wally Festschrift, our new boss. Wally is a gigantic, sloppy, fat genius who loves his work. "Hot shot detective agency presidents like me don' usually work Sat'days," he said. "But anything good enough to cut a honeymoon short is good enough for me. I'll be here when you get here. An' remember, Phil, be careful. When Wally ain't along, the cats will play, or somethin'."

Or somethin', is right, I thought, laughing.

With time to kill, Margo and I planned our next day. We had paid in advance and would just leave the keys in an envelope on the porch. The friend who loaned me the four-wheel drive didn't mind the prospect of getting up early the next morning because he had been looking for a graceful way to see if the car would, by any stroke of luck, be available earlier than we'd planned.

It was getting late, but we had a lot of packing and tidying up to do before we got to sleep. The pay phone rang.

"Yeah."

"Mr. Spence?"

"Yeah, Meaghan, you all set?"

"No, I'm scared!"

"What's up?"

"He's been here! I'm calling from the lobby. He's been in my room. He ransacked all my stuff. He didn't take anything, not even some money I left in there, but he must have been looking for something. I don't want to stay here. Please come and get me!"

I took her number and promised to call back soon. Margo and I didn't know what to do. The honeymoon was shot by now. There was little more we could salvage of that, and that wasn't the issue.

Could we run to Meaghan without tipping our hand and losing our chance of finding out who was stalking her and what he wanted?

"Can we take the chance of leaving her there and hoping he won't come back?" Margo asked.

"I don't know. We don't even know for sure it was that guy who ransacked the room, but of course, if no money was taken, it wasn't just a petty larceny. What if it *was* him and he thinks she's got whatever he was looking for the first time?"

"Right. We'd better go get her."

"No, we'd better let her come to us again. There's still a chance this guy doesn't know where she's been. We can determine whether she's been followed, and if she hasn't, maybe we can get her checked in somewhere else."

"Just for another night alone?" Margo asked.

"No. I just think we should show up at the airport separate from her tomorrow and that we shouldn't be seen with her any more than necessary before that. Although another night alone isn't a bad fringe benefit."

Meaghan didn't much like the idea of going back to her room and packing her stuff, but she did save a night's charge by complaining about the lack of security. The management offered to give her another room free, but she declined and took a cab back to the laundromat.

We waited around awhile and then drove in circles, but it was apparent no one was following us. By the time we had Meaghan checked in to another place, it was well after midnight. And by the time we were packed and ready to just hit the road in the morning, we had only a few hours to sleep.

Even getting to Logan Airport early didn't help us get seats together in coach. The irony was that they said they had a couple of seats together in first class if we wanted to upgrade our tickets again. It was tempting, but all of a sudden the return trip was business, not pleasure, and we declined.

"Would you believe we're newlyweds who can't find two seats together?" Margo asked the man on the aisle next to me in coach.

"Sure, hey, I'll believe anything *you* tell me, sweetie."

I stared at him, wondering if he hadn't realized she was referring to me as half of that newlywed couple.

"No offense kid," he said, quickly, "but you're a lucky guy."

"Yeah, I know," I muttered.

"I'd even move to a center seat for *this* young lady," he said, trying to stand before unlatching his seat belt, causing him to slam back down into the seat. He swore. And then he moved. Margo thanked him.

For twenty-five minutes we craned our necks to see if Meaghan had arrived. The in-flight supervisor, who had identified herself as Carole Moffatt, ran through the safety features, the other attendants pantomiming as she spoke. When she got to the part about our being sure that our "seat backs and tray tables are in their full upright position for take off," we saw Meaghan scurrying down the aisle with her luggage, wearing a fatigued, embarrassed smile for the rest of the staff, and not looking at the passengers, not even us. That was a good girl. For a while we had wondered what we had gotten ourselves into.

"None of the men's nametags say 'Dwayne,'" Margo said. "The black one is a Walter and the other is a Fred."

A few minutes later, a note from Meaghan with our first soft drinks explained it. "My hotel didn't have a courtesy car. Almost missed the flight. Dwayne is on vacation. Carole is the tall, pretty one. My 'friend' is in 22B. I'm glad you're here."

We shouldn't have been any more surprised than Meaghan that her man was on board, but I was. For some reason, I didn't expect to see him. "He's got to have unbelievable connections," Margo said. "She reaches someone in the middle of the night who straightens everything out and gets her reassigned, and this guy somehow knows it. He's got to be hooked in with the airline somehow, Philip."

I nodded, wondering. The first chance I got, I mosied back toward the lavatory, casually watching seat numbers as I went.The man in 22B looked to be about five-foot ten-inches tall and of average weight, but he was stuffed into a loud Hawaiian-type shirt and black pants that made him look a little tubby. He had a two- or three-day growth of beard and his hair was greasy and slicked back. I couldn't get a look at his finger, but I assumed Meaghan had. I tried to sneak another peek on the way back, but I had no more luck, except to notice his blue and white sneakers.

"When we get off in Chicago," I told Margo, "I'm going to buck the traffic and go to the back, as if to get a bag or something, and then while he's following Meaghan, I can follow *him*. Wait for me downstairs at baggage claim near the limo dispatchers, but ignore all their pitches. They're just there to steal each other's reserved riders."

"You in the mood for a little advice?"

"I'll be careful, love."

"Not that. Well, that and something else, Philip. He's not going to be following anyone surreptitiously in *that* getup. He'll have time to duck in somewhere and change before the flight crew is even off the plane. Keep an eye on him. Don't expect the guy who goes into the washroom to be the one who comes out."

"Anybody ever tell you you'd make a decent detective?"

I badly misjudged how long it would take me to get to the back of the plane and then catch up with the man I was supposed to be following. When I turned around to head back up to the head of the plane, I was probably twenty or so people behind the man.

I looked way ahead and saw Margo staring back at me as she headed out the door. She briefly brushed her finger past her temple, as if pointing at her eye. I assumed she meant she would keep an eye on him until I got out, but I wished she wouldn't. We were going to look obvious if we weren't careful, and I wasn't sure how crucial it was that we keep a close tail on him that day anyway. What we needed to do was to connect with Meaghan somewhere and be sure she was all right.

When I reached the front of the plane, I was among the last few people aboard. Meaghan maneuvered her way near me and bent down to drag a suitcase from the closet. "How long before you deplane?" I asked quickly.

"Just a few minutes," she said. "See you in the parking lot?"

I nodded and hurried off. As I merged with all the foot traffic heading toward the ticket counters and the escalators down to baggage claim, I saw Margo standing about fifty feet ahead of me, staring intently at the TV monitors that announce arrivals and departures for TransCoastal and all the rest.

I slowed and kept my eyes on her until she turned toward me. Looking me dead in the face, and with a look of resolve and—I thought—encouragement, she formed her right hand into the shape of a gun and pointed directly into the men's washroom just ahead of me. He'd gone in there? I slowed and motioned to the door with my head. She nodded, turned, and headed away.

I backed off and took a vantage point about twenty feet behind the men's washroom exit, remembering Margo's advice. I couldn't be too sure the guy who went in would look at all like the one who would come out.

Chapter Four

I was guessing that the stubble-faced, Hawaiian-shirted man had been in the washroom less than two minutes by the time Margo tipped me off. Was he really five-ten, or had it been a mistake to try to judge his height while he was seated?

In the next thirty seconds, the only men to emerge were a hefty young man in a Navy uniform, two airline workers in utility outfits with ear silencers hooked to their belts, and a middle-aged priest wearing wire-rim glasses.

I watched him carefully, because he carried no luggage. Had he checked *all* his bags? Ah, he was legit. He hurried to catch up to three other priests, and I turned my attention back to the washroom door.

Now I was confused. Several people went in and out, fathers with their sons, execs, cowboys. None looked like my man, but I just didn't know anymore. By now I was sure he wouldn't look the same coming out as he had going in, but I didn't want to overestimate the change either.

Could Margo have been wrong? Could *Meaghan* have even been wrong? Had I seen the right man she was trying to point out on the plane?

And then here came Meaghan. Of course! Whoever it was wouldn't leave the washroom until she had passed, would he?

She caught my eye and winked. I clenched a fist of greeting so only she—and not the friends with her—would notice.

I grew nervous when two more full minutes passed with no one emerging from the washroom who could possibly be my mark. I finally decided I'd better check it out and see if he'd slipped me. As soon as I pushed open the washroom door I knew he wasn't there. A fast survey of the area showed just a couple of men, neither close to his description. How had he done it?

I pushed open the swinging door on the trash can near the exit and found a cheap green and red plaid shoulder bag, zipped shut. My heart sank when I pulled it open. There was the loud shirt, the sneakers, a tiny can of shaving cream, and a disposable razor.

I blasted through the exit door and ran down the corridor, passing bunches of people and scaring many coming the other way. It wasn't unusual to see people running *toward* the planes, but *from* them?

Crazily, I was hoping to recognize someone I remembered coming out that door, but who, which one? Someone who had cut himself shaving so fast? I ran past the three priests and realized that they had been ahead of Meaghan. What had I done, run past *her?* What must she have thought? Now she was unprotected!

I slid to a stop and ran back the other way. When Meaghan came into view I could see the terror in her eyes. She had to think something big was coming down, but she couldn't ask me, she couldn't run, she didn't know, she couldn't do anything.

Three priests? There had been four when the one

in the washroom caught up with them! Why were there only three now? Was that my man? He had black pants. All he would have needed was a new top, a change of shoes, and a fast shave.

But why would he have come out ahead of Meaghan? Was running into the three priests just a stroke of luck that allowed him to walk with them a while before he ducked into another waiting area to wait for Meaghan to come by? That could be the only explanation. I hoped.

Breathless, I changed direction once more and sprinted back to the three priests. I didn't even want to see Meaghan's reaction this time.

"Excuse me, Fathers," I said, gasping and causing them all to stop and—no doubt—wonder if there was some emergency. "But weren't there four of you?"

They looked at each other. "I beg your pardon," the eldest said gently.

"Weren't there four of you walking together just a few minutes ago? Back there."

"Uh, well, we met a colleague from the Chicago diocese who was on his way to a connecting flight. He merely greeted us and then left us when he arrived at his gate."

"Do you remember which gate or where he was going?"

Now I had gone too far. They were beginning to look annoyed. "No, I don't recall," the older said. "I don't believe he told us. Is there some way one of us can help you, or will you excuse us?"

"I'm sorry, sir. Could you just tell me if you knew this man, this other priest, the one you said was a colleague?"

They'd heard enough and began to move away. "No, I had not met him before. We're from New York."

"Did you get his name?"

"No!"

I didn't want to run past Meaghan again, so I quickly bought a paper from one of the machines and sat pretending to read it by the windows in front of the ticket counters. When Meaghan and Carole and another flight attendant came by, pulling their luggage behind them, I was certain Meaghan missed me. Anyone following her would have to come by me, and I had a perfect view of the corridor leading from the gates to the counter area, which also led to the escalators to the baggage area and to the parking garage.

As Meaghan and her friends started down the escalator to my left, I saw my man emerge from the corridor, but he didn't head left past me; he went to the right, around the back of the counter area where the metal detectors for the other gate corridor were located.

I stood as he moved out of my vision. Had I completely blown this? Could he really be a Chicago priest who just happened to see some brothers of the cloth when he emerged from the washroom? That would mean I had missed the man on the plane from seat 22B. But no! The "priest" had told the New Yorkers he had a plane to catch in the same corridor, and now here he was, heading around the other side of the ticket counter area.

Maybe I was wrong; maybe he was just looking to buy a magazine or a souvenir, or maybe his flight had been reassigned, but I had no other leads and I wasn't going to let him slip through my fingers.

I hurried around to the other side and saw him ahead of me by about forty-five feet. I slowed to let him lengthen his lead a bit. Sure enough, he knew where he was going. He bypassed the corridor to the other gates. He ignored the food and trinket shops. He reached the other end, where he could have continued to yet another set of gates, but he took a left around the far end of the ticket counters again and took the first escalator down to the baggage area. I knew he hadn't seen me, so I sped to catch up, boarding the escalator a few steps behind him.

He glanced at his watch and took three steps down before letting the machine carry him the rest of the way. Either I had drowned in a sea of fantasy or this man was a pro. That escalator brought him into view of Meaghan just as she turned into the little alcove leading to the stairs down to the parking garage elevators.

I decided to stay close, even running the risk of his noticing, and his first mistake came at the elevators to the parking garage. He let too much distance come between himself and Meaghan, and even jogging a few steps didn't get him close enough to her to put him on the same elevator. Here would have been a benign, middle-aged priest coming into her view for the first time, yet who had likely been following Meaghan for weeks, trailing her to Boston, ransacking her hotel room for who knows what, and still trying to stay close enough to follow her—I assumed—by car. Well, if he was going to follow her, I was going to follow him.

When the elevator doors closed, despite the efforts of an elderly passenger who had seen the trotting priest at the last minute and had vainly searched for the *door open* button, the priest looked around, hesitated briefly upon seeing only me, and dashed for the door to the stairs. Apparently he didn't know which floor Meaghan's car was on, and I figured he wanted to charge up to each floor and see if she got off. But then how would he be able to get to his car quickly enough to follow her? Anyway, our plan was that Meaghan should meet *us* in the parking lot. She was going to wait at the elevators for us at the fourth level, and here was my man, bounding up the stairs!

If I followed him, even from a distance, I'd give myself away. He'd be able to hear the loud echoes of someone running in those stairways behind him. But I couldn't let him get to Meaghan without me there. We were assuming he had the gun Meaghan had seen on the Wednesday morning flight, and I didn't have mine, but still I would never be able to forgive myself if I couldn't do *something*, even by just showing up.

I knew that by running at top speed—which he could do if he was in shape, and I had a feeling that whoever this guy was, he was professional enough to be in excellent condition—he would beat the elevator, and thus Meaghan (and me), to the fourth level. When another elevator popped open, I jumped on and pushed the *door close* button as quickly as I could, shutting the car just as other travelers dragged their luggage up to it, cursing me. I was sorry, but I didn't feel I had a choice.

I rode to the fifth level and ran to the door to the stairs, opening it far enough to stick my head in. I heard fast footsteps on the stairs, then a door opening and closing. What was going on? Assuming he was no longer in the stairwell, I flew down two and three steps at a time to the fourth level where Meaghan was waiting. She was startled to see me.

"Mr. Spence, what is it? What's going on?"

"I'm not sure yet, but listen, take the next elevator down and go directly to Margo at the TransCoastal baggage claim area. I want you both to wait there. I'm not sure when I'll be back, but I'll come there for you. There's an elevator, grab it! Meaghan, listen, what floor did your friends get off at?"

"I don't know, ah, five or six I think. They were still on when I got off."

"Better yet," I said, "tell me what kind of a car Carole drives."

Meaghan was trying to think quickly before the elevator doors closed. "Oh, uh, it's one of those expensive gray things, like a Mercedes only not quite."

"A Volvo?"

"Yeah, no. A, um, BMC or something like that." And the door closed.

I ran to my car, hands shaking, trying to dig my keys out, open the door, start the car, back it up, and pull away all in one motion. It can't be done. I'm not sure what I did to the transmission, let alone the tires, with that move, but I sure made a lot of noise. I screeched down the spiral ramps the way I wish parking lot attendants wouldn't.

When I got to the pay booths I had no idea if I had beaten either Carole or my man, and I didn't know either if my hunch was right that he had switched and was now following *her*. I pulled off to the side, grabbed a map from the glove box, and stood outside the car with it spread on the hood.

A few seconds later, Carole and the other flight attendant drove past in a gray BMW. I squinted and stared at each car in the pay booths. To me, any one of the drivers could have been my man, even one of the women, but I didn't figure he'd had time to do anything but ditch the turned-back collar.

I waited about half an hour and assumed I had either missed him or that he was still waiting for Meaghan's car to emerge. Unless he had slipped past me, I decided he was following only Meaghan, not Carole.

I drove back around the loop and stopped downstairs in front of the TransCoastal baggage claim area. "I think it'll be worth the safety of it if we drive Meaghan to her car and then follow her to her apartment," I said, filling them in on my little escapade and trying to make sense of it.

"You think this guy, the priest, is waiting in the garage somewhere for Meaghan to leave?" Margo asked.

"Either that or he got tired of waiting and he's coming this way or has given up for the day. I don't think I saw him after I saw Carole and the other girl leave."

"Stacy," Meaghan said. "She's not from our crew. She was just filling in, until they could find me, that is. Nice girl. She's into that Fellowship of Christian Airline Personnel or whatever they call it." Margo caught my eye, but it wasn't the time to change subjects.

"We want you to meet our boss and get his ideas on all this," I said. "But I imagine you want to go home first and be sure you're not being followed." She nodded. "But if we follow you home and you ride back with us, whoever is following you will be onto us. Why don't we follow you until you're safely in your place, then we'll see you at our offices for a late lunch, say around two?"

As we followed Meaghan's car out of the parking garage and up to the pay booth, I spotted my priest pulling the same stunt I had tried, only in a different location. "That's him, Margo! Over there! And he's still got the collar on. He's spotted Meaghan's car. Now watch, he'll fold up the map and get back in his car."

I glided left into the booth next to Meaghan and exited at almost the same time. I held back, waiting to see what he would do. He was driving a wood-grain-sided late model station wagon, and he casually fell in about three cars behind Meaghan in her lane. I let him pass, noting the license number and stayed several car lengths behind him and to his left.

We maintained those relative positions all the way to the Ohio Street exit ramp off the Kennedy, where we shortened the gaps at each light until Meaghan turned right onto Michigan Avenue. He crossed us up by continuing straight, but I assumed he would come around the other way and pick her up again before she reached her apartment building. When she pulled into her underground parking garage, I waited at the curb a couple of blocks away, looking for the station wagon. It never showed. I wondered if he had caught onto me.

"Give her a call, please, Mar," I said. "See if she's OK and tell her we'll see her later."

Margo called her from a nearby phone booth and

hurried back to the car. "She's glad we followed her. She seemed unaware of the priest in the station wagon, so I didn't say anything. No sense upsetting her more. She's convinced someone was in her apartment while she was gone, but she can't put a finger on why she thinks so. Nothing has been disturbed. Just a feeling, she said."

"I'm beginning to trust her feelings, if you know what I mean," I said.

"I sure do. Philip, this is a strange one, you've gotta admit."

"Worth shortening the honeymoon for, Nancy Drew?" I said, heading north to Glencoe. "Remember, that was *your* idea."

She turned to look at me, waiting until I stole a glance at her. She smiled. "Nothing can shorten *our* honeymoon, sweetheart. It'll never end."

One of the last items cared for by Earl Haymeyer, owner of both the EH Detective Agency and the Glencoe building that housed it, was to rent Margo and me a bigger apartment, down the hall a few doors from where I had lived for quite a while. We hated to just dump our stuff in the place when we arrived, because we had worked so hard to make it homey during the few weeks before our wedding. But Wally was waiting, coming in on a "Sat'day," as he called it, just because of us, and we knew he'd have to get his leering craziness out of the way before we could get down to business.

What the office had lacked by having a dapper, classy, highly organized and efficient boss in Earl Haymeyer was easily made up for by Walvoord Feinberg Festschrift, former Sergeant of Detectives in the Chicago Police Department's Homicide Division. Wally had none of what Earl had, except that he was all cop. And there was no one Earl respected more in the profession than Wally Festschrift.

"So don't expect a clean desk, everything in it's place, and everything right with the world," Earl had warned us. "Do expect to work long and hard and fast, and remember, my name is still on the door. Wally may appear a little frayed around the edges, but I'm proud to have him running the place for at least a few years, and you will be too. You can learn as much from him as you did from me, if not more."

Wally would have had to go some to match what we learned from Earl, but we had both worked a couple of cases with Wally, and he *was* a piece of work in action.

In the short time we'd been gone, he'd dragged all of Earl's furniture out of his office and set it in the middle of the outer offices where Margo's and my desks were, along with one recently vacated by a former associate, and the reception area where Bonnie Murray took care of us all day. We couldn't imagine what Wally had in mind for Earl's old office; we already had a darkroom.

"Oh, that'll be a private conference room," he explained, after welcoming us back with nothing but a silent, knowing, ear-to-ear grin. "I don' like bein' separated from the troops. I liked Earl's furnishings, but not his digs, you know what I mean?"

We nodded, also smiling knowingly, trying to look ahead to what it would be like to have the boss right out in the middle of everything. In the backs of our minds I think we thought we could control Wally's creative housekeeping if we could keep him cooped up in the big private office.

"I know it looks a little more like a newspaper office, with the editor in the middle and all his people on the rim, but I like it, don' you? It's gonna be nice. We'll all work together, learn from each other, huh? Good, right?"

We nodded again. Yeah, it probably would be good. Fun, if nothing else.

"So, let's go get somethin' to eat, kids, how 'bout it? I'm dyin' here."

"Oh, I'm sorry, Wally," Margo said. "The girl we told you about, Meaghan Hanekamp, is coming at about two, and we promised her we'd wait and have a late lunch with her."

Wally looked pained. "You gotta be kiddin'! That's two hours!" He paced around a little, as if thinking it over. "Awright, you already got me in here on a Sat'day; we mi's well make it miserable. Tell me about this stewardess girl."

"She's called a flight attendant," I said, proud of my newfound knowledge.

"Whatever," Wally said, rolling his eyes. "See if you can tell me about her over my growling stomach."

Chapter Five

When Meaghan arrived a little before two, we knew something had gotten to Wally. He quit griping about his hunger and seemed preoccupied, maybe even troubled. After the introductions, Margo asked if he wanted her to have something sent up, sandwiches or anything.

"Nah, let's get this lady signed up here so we can get a few questions answered, unless *you* people are hungry."

Unless we were hungry? We were famished.

"Well, I sort of am," Meaghan admitted cautiously. "I was too nervous to eat on the flight."

"Me too, Wally," Margo said.

"Yeah," I added, "how about letting one of us order something?"

"Awright, but make it quick. Get me a couple of the big sandwiches, whatever the joint's specialty is. Why don't you two go get it to save time, and I'll get this agency form filled out with Miss Hanekamp here. We gotta get a little better acquainted anyway, don't we, girl?"

Meaghan smiled shyly and nodded, glancing nervously at us. Margo squeezed her shoulder on the way out.

"What is going *on* with Wally?" she asked in the car.

"I wish I knew. He seems so different."

"Different isn't the word for it, Philip. We struck a nerve somewhere with that story. It's almost as if we offended him or something. Did I say something that should have bothered him?"

"Not that I heard. Did I?"

"No. I just don't understand. It was as if we pulled his plug. He quit asking questions like he usually does, and—"

"Yeah, he usually interrupts with so many questions you can't get your story out. At what point in the story did that happen, do you recall?"

"Well, it seems he was normal until we talked about how Meaghan knew it was the same guy every time. Do you suppose maybe he thinks that's a little weak and he doesn't want to hurt us by telling us we should have seen through it?"

"An overabundance of tact is not one of Wally Festschrift's faults, Margo. He would have come right out with that one. No, I thought he started clamming up when we talked about actually seeing the guy for ourselves. I got the impression maybe he didn't think all those coincidences necessarily proved the guy was who we thought he was, and that even if he was, that it didn't mean he was tailing Meaghan."

"Is it possible Wally doesn't even believe *her* story and doesn't think we should, either?"

"Anything's possible, but you know he'll tell us straight when she's gone. He always does."

"Oh, yes. He does tell us straight. Which should remind you of something. Remember the last time he came to church with us?"

"Yeah, he sure told us straight that time, didn't he?"

"Right, so what does that remind you of?"

"You mean other than that he was a little upset and said so? I'll bite. What should it remind me of?"

"When did he say he'd come to church with us again?"

"That's right! When we're celebrating our one-week anniversary! That's tomorrow! I wonder if he remembers?"

"Of course he won't, Philip, but have you ever known him to back out of a deal?"

"No, but I've never known him quite so angry as when he thought the pastor was speaking right to him that night, either."

"It didn't bother Earl, and I thought we convinced Wally that it wasn't personal unless he took it that way."

"Ah, now you're the one with the bad memory. What you told him, Mar, was more along the lines of 'if the shoe fits, wear it.' "

"Ouch. Do you think so, Philip?"

"Yes, ma'am."

"Maybe I'd better go easy on making him follow through on his promise to go with us tomorrow."

"Yes, ma'am. Go easy, but—"

"But don't let him off the hook."

"Right."

We bought a bunch of stuff from Al's Froggy Deli, surprising Meaghan with one of our favorites, and taking the safe route with Wally by presenting him with two "Croaker Chokers." Though he pretended to be too intrigued with Meaghan's story to eat, he snarfed those monsters down and waterfalled them into oblivion under a quart of Coke. "Not bad," he said, lifting his stubby legs onto his new desk and nearly tipping himself over backwards. He interlocked his fingers behind his head and looked as if he were about to be launched, but apparently he was comfortable, because he asked Meaghan to continue telling him about her co-workers. What he was onto, we didn't know. We'd have to ask later.

"So you wouldn't say you were particularly close to this Carole?"

"No, sir. I mean, I've never been to her house or anything like that. She asked me early on, as I told you, but I never went because she made it sound like there would be this wild stuff going on and everything."

"What's everything?"

"Sir?"

"You said 'wild stuff and everything.' I was wonderin' what *everything* was."

"Oh, I don't know. Everything everything. Drinking, men, whatever."

"You got a problem with men? You put men and drinking in the same bag?"

"Well, no, not in a bad way—"

"You say you don't want to go to a co-worker's place because there'll be wild stuff and everything, making the everything sound as bad as the wild stuff, and then you tell me that the everything includes drinking and men but that that doesn't put men and drinking in a bad light? You a drinker, Miss, uh—"

"Hanekamp," Margo helped. Meaghan was speechless. Wally was in rare form, and we felt sorry for the little girl. We'd learned not to interrupt him when he was on a roll, however, because he was usually pushing for something specific, whether it appeared that way or not.

"I'm not above a little wine with dinner," she said, only slightly defensively. "But I've never been drunk, and I don't go to parties just to drink."

"And you're not above a little date now and then, but you've never been in love and—"

"That's right," Meaghan said, quick on the draw this time. "If you're going to get personal, that's exactly right, and I'm the type who's saving myself for the right guy, however that sounds."

"That sounds awright to me, honey," Wally said, and we could tell he was about to ease off and get to his point. But Meaghan couldn't tell.

"Well, I don't see how it's any of your business, and if you really want to help me, you'd ask about this man who's been following me and—"

"I'll get to him, Miss Hanekamp," Wally said, suddenly soothing. "But let me tell you something. Things are rarely as they seem. I may not be the best judge of character, but there's more to you than you're letting on. I gotta know what it is. I gotta find out if it's true that you're not close to the people you work with, and I also gotta know, if it *is* true, if it's because of their parties-with-the-wild-stuff-and-everything you're so worried about or something else that keeps the distance there."

"What are you saying?"

"I'm saying that this person following you, whoever he is, is a professional. He's not following you because you're a wonderful, Four-H type kid who's never been into anything more than a little wine before dinner. Now, maybe you're telling me the truth, and maybe there's nothing in your background that would make me want to think of you as the type of person who *should* be followed around by people who apparently know what they're doing. If that's not the case, dear, you'd better tell me now. Because if you don't tell me, and there's something there you don't want me to find out, you can just bet your life that it'll be the first thing I find. If there's a *reason* this guy—low-life or pro, whichever—is on your tail, then maybe I don't wanna know who he is *or* help get him out of your life."

Well, it was vintage Wally Festschrift. He had his own way of screening clients, and he had succeeded in moving Meaghan, and almost Margo, to tears. I could tell Margo was restraining herself from demanding to know what he was up to without apparent cause. Instead she turned her attention to comforting Meaghan.

"I don't need *this*," Meaghan was saying. "I go and finally take the step to get some help, and I get accused of being some sort of a, a—"

"He's not accusing you, Meaghan," Margo said. "He just has to know everything, just like a lawyer would, if we're going to—"

"Just like a lawyer all right, but for which side? I feel like he's—"

"Let me defend myself here, Margo," Wally said, standing and uncharacteristically putting a hand on Meaghan's shoulder. "Young lady," he said, "you're gonna learn to like ol' Wally a lot. Because if you're straight—even if you're not as straight as you'd like us to think you are—I'm gonna wanna find this creep and take care of him for ya."

Meaghan tried to smile, but Wally wheeled a chair directly in front of her, sat heavily so he was almost knee to knee with her, and continued.

"On the other hand, if you've got any secrets, you

better tell me now, because I'm not braggin', but nobody I've ever known has been able to keep much from me very long."

He looked up at Margo and me for confirmation. We were both nodding already. Meaghan appeared frightened. "I lied about a homework project in junior high," she said, and Wally roared.

"This girl just might be as straight as she thinks she is!"

"And I'm chaste," she said. "You can ask anyone."

Wally was nearly in tears. "Well, girl," he said, pausing to let one more guffaw escape, "that's not the type of thing I was gonna investigate. But unless your villain is a junior high truant officer or represents all the frustrated guys in your life who've tried to get next to you, you're gonna hafta give me a little something more to go on."

Now Meaghan was embarrassed and not sure what to say. "I'm your typical oldest child from a pretty normal family," she said. "There's nothing bad or mysterious or even exciting that ever happened to me. I was the only girl from my hometown to ever become a flight attendant, and you'd have thought I'd become Miss America. They had a day for me at the high school, picture on the front page of the paper, everything. But that's it. Nothing else."

"Awright," Wally said. "Let's get down to business. You ever do any dope?"

"No."

"Not even a little grass?"

"No."

"Smoke a cigarette?"

Meaghan hesitated. "No."

Wally squinted at her. "C'mon! I don't think I know *any* adult who never *once* took a drag on a cigarette."

"Well, I tried one once when I was alone, but nobody ever knew that and I never told anybody before, and now you've made me say it in front of three people. What kind of a person are you, anyway?"

"Did you inhale?"

"What *are* you talking about?"

"I wanna know if maybe you took a drag or two and blew the smoke out and then you wondered if maybe the reason you couldn't taste it or that it was no big deal the way your friends said was because you hadn't actually breathed it in. And so you inhaled the next time and you came up coughing, and when you put it out and stood up, you thought all you felt was guilt until you tried to walk into the next room, then you felt lightheaded and had to sit down again. That's when you realized you never should have done it and you vowed you'd never do it again. And you probably haven't."

Meaghan hid her face in her hands. "Why are you doing this to me?"

"That's how it was, wasn't it? Where was I wrong? Anywhere? Maybe you coughed the first time or got sick before you stood up, or maybe you *were* sick and dizziness had nothing to do with it?"

"No, no, you were exactly right the first time. That's exactly the way it happened. But how did you know, and what does it have to do with this guy following me all over the country?"

"It has nothin' to do with anyone followin' you, kid, but you're gonna learn to tell me everything, the truth the first time out of the chute, because there are things I know that you don't go to college to learn. You think Philip or Margo didn't have the same smoking experience you did? You think *I* didn't? Baby, we've all had that experience, so don't lay any baloney on me. I been around too long. And if you think it stops with knowing what it was like when you copped your first drag on a cigarette, well, we haven't even started yet."

"What do you mean?"

"I mean I wanna know why you left your previous crew? You just wanted new surroundings? No problems with the other crew?"

"No."

"No?"

"No!"

"No romantic troubles? No guy on the crew that you really liked but maybe you found out he was off limits? Maybe you found out he was married or gay? Or maybe there was a second or third man in the cockpit who was tryin' to hustle you, 'cept he was married. An' instead of just politely shutting him down, you maybe got him in trouble by telling somebody who could make it difficult for him? Maybe the other girls on the crew were having the same trouble with him, but you were the only one who came forward and complained, so from then on you were shunned. They were all glad you did what you did, but they didn't wanna associate with a snitch? What was it, Meaghan? What was the problem with the last crew, and the one before that?"

Meaghan sobbed. "Are you just pulling all this out of a hat? I didn't tell Margo or Mr. Spence any of this. Who told you this?"

"Is it not true? Any of it?"

"Most of it *is* true, but I still don't know how you know and what difference it makes. This guy following me has nothing to do with any of that."

Wally slowed his pace and became parental again. "The fact is, dear, I *was* pulling that out of a hat. I'm not tryin' to show you what a great mind-reader I am or anything like that. I just know human nature. I know why people change jobs, change locations, and all that. I just want you to get the point that you can't snow me, and so far you're still hiding the little stuff from me. What's that s'posed to make us think about the big things you may be hiding, the things that may be causing you to be followed? Now, maybe there isn't anything bigger than a lie and a cigarette here and a squeal there, but if there is, I remind you, you can tell us, or we'll dig it up."

Meaghan wiped her eyes and faced Wally. "If you'll give me some time, I'll think about what you've said here. Right now I feel a little pressured, and it's not the way I expected to be made to feel by the people I thought were going to help me."

"But you understand that that wasn't my point, don't you?"

"I think so, but there is one thing I'd like to straighten out."

"Sure."

"I didn't fall for any gay guy, but there was one on the crew I worked for."

Wally appeared puzzled. Was the girl actually this naive? Did she think Wally was omniscient and that she had to clarify the small points of his forays into her psyche? "Not that it makes any difference," Wally said, "but did you get him in trouble too?"

"No. After I reported the navigator for coming on to me and everyone else, LeRoy told me he was sorry he had ever told me he was gay and begged me not to tell anyone. He made me tell him whether I would report him or not. I told him I didn't think there was any regulation or law against *being* a homosexual, but that if I knew he had approached a passenger or a crew member, yes, I would have to report him."

"You enjoy trouble that much?"

"No, I was just raised that way. You do what's right. You do your duty. I answered the question in the oral exam at flight attendant school that way too. They wanted to know if you would do what was right even if it cost you your friends. I said yes."

"And you meant it."

"Yes I did."

"And so what did LeRoy say to that?"

"He said I was sick. You can guess by the way I was raised what I thought about an admitted homosexual calling *me* sick."

Wally chuckled. "Yeah, I imagine I can." He rose again. "You had enough for one day, young lady?"

"Yes, sir."

"Then let me ask you just one more thing, if you don't mind. Do you have any idea, any idea at all, whether it makes sense or not, why anyone would follow you around?"

"None."

"Now just wait a minute, sweetie. That's not the kind of question you can answer quickly. I didn't ask you if anything came to you off the top of your head. I asked you whether you could think of *anything at all* that would result in the kind of hassle you've been going through."

Meaghan stood and paced. "I'm sorry," she said. "I really can't, Mr. Festschrift."

"When's your next flight?"

"Monday afternoon."

"Perfect. We have a regular Monday morning staff meeting, and then someone from here will be on board with you. OK?"

"Then you believe me? You don't doubt me or wonder about me?"

"I wonder about everybody, lady. We'll talk more next week. If you need us over the weekend, you have our number."

Margo walked Meaghan down to her car, and as soon as they were out of sight, Wally slammed his fist on the desktop and swore. I jumped. He walked quickly back and forth in front of the window, watching for Margo to return. He stopped and stared down to the parking lot and muttered, almost under his breath, "C'mon, Margo, don't chat now. Ah, here she comes."

He met Margo at the top of the stairs and opened the door for her, signaling where we both should sit. She looked puzzled, and I *knew* I was. When we were both seated, Wally kept walking as he talked. "You're buyin' her package, aren't you," he said, agitated. "I'll admit she's good, one of the best I've seen."

I looked at Margo. "If you mean do we believe her," she said, "yes, I think we do. But I don't want to speak for Philip. For myself, I believe every word. You worked her pretty hard, Wally, and except for a few evidences of naivete, I thought she held up fairly well."

Wally looked hopefully to me, but I nodded and he turned away. "I know the guy who's following her," he said.

"You *know* him?" Margo repeated, incredulous.

"If it's who I think it is, and I'm sure it is, yes. His name is Jules Perkins. He got his little finger torn up in a pistol firing mechanism malfunction when he was with the Illinois Bureau of Investigation. You know who he's with now? The Federal Narcotics Bureau."

"What are you saying, Wally?"

"I'm sayin' I'm afraid your Little Miss Goodie Two Shoes has either been mistaken for someone else, or she's up to her ears in interstate trafficking of controlled substances. Perkins wouldn't be involved unless she was a big-time dope peddler."

Chapter Six

Margo and I were still in shock by the next morning when it was time to pick Wally up for church. He had grumpily remembered his promise to Margo.

"I didn't think you kids would be back from your honeymoon on your one week's anniversary," he said.

"You don't have to go, Wally," Margo told him.

"Sure, an' then you got it hangin' over my head forever that I backed out of a deal? Forget it."

Wally looked as he usually did when he felt the occasion demanded it. He was in his least rumpled suit, fortunately the one where the pant legs were long enough to cover his white socks, even when the belt was pulled up to waist level, which it now wasn't.

"We don't want you to come just because you said you would," Margo said. "In fact, we never want you to come unless you want to."

"Awright, I want to, OK? I'm a sucker for pretty zealots, fair enough? Anyways, ol' Haymeyer scares me to death gettin' religion from you two, and better than that, he was tryin' to pawn it off on me before he's actually got it himself."

We were silent. We'd been through it before. He knew Haymeyer hadn't gotten "religion" and also that whatever he got he didn't get from us. Wally just liked to wade in and say all the things he knew we'd want to counter, just so he wouldn't appear like too easy a mark.

We, on the other hand, had learned so much from Earl about how to—and more importantly, how not to—try to effectively tell our friends what a personal God could mean to them, that we began resisting the urge to argue with Wally every time he tried to raise our hackles by referring to it as "getting religion," calling us "zealots," and pretending that he was being dragged kicking and screaming into the church.

I must admit, it was funny to see him in what he considered a formal situation. If he'd looked around when he walked into the sanctuary, he would have seen that not everyone was even dressed up, let alone formally. There were enough young people and people of modest means and people from nearly every walk of life that Wally should have been able to see that—within reason—he could have worn what he wanted and been somewhat more casual during the service.

But from some childhood memory, Wally carted along an image of a church that was stuffy and formal and severe. He'd start getting nervous when we pulled into the parking lot.

"No wonder Haymeyer quit goin' here and started goin' to your old church, Philip. This one's too small. No place to hide. Everybody knows your business."

Well, Earl had merely developed a fondness for the style and grace of the pastor at my former church, and when I switched to Margo's church, Earl continued going to mine—a fact I was unaware of until he announced that he had become a Christian and told us all about it.

The irony of it was that it was Wally who had made a deal with us—in Earl's *and* his behalf—that they would come to church with us again. Earl had resisted what we tried to tell him for many months, then he seemed to soften. And when his old love/hate friend, Wally Festschrift, came back into his life, Earl knew that here was a man who needed what we'd been talking about for so long, even though Earl himself had taken no personal action on it. Earl had taken Wally under his wing, told him all about forgiveness of sin, changed lives, getting to know God personally through Christ, the whole picture.

One of the things Earl always made clear was that he could not be badgered, pushed, cajoled, whatever, into becoming a Christian. He considered it a very personal and private matter, at least until he did take the step. That was when he realized he had many brothers and sisters in Christ and that there was a certain thrill in letting them know that he was one of the family now.

Oddly, Earl's decision to believe seemed to coincide with his feeling that it was time to back off on his efforts with Wally. "He's right where I was," Earl told us. "He's heard enough. He knows the score. He's at a point where he might tell his friends about this—the way I did—but you're not going to push him over the line any more than you did me. Just keep letting him know you care, invite him to church, all that, but lighten up on the pressure. He'll come around."

It was true enough that Earl and Wally were a lot alike, whether they looked or acted it or not.

"Nobody knows your business," Margo told Wally as we emerged from the car. "All they know is that you're our friend and that we work with you."

"Yeah? I bet they already know I'm the new boss."

"So what's wrong with that?" I said.

"Nothing," he said, grinning. "I was just checking to make sure they knew at least that." He grew sullen again. "They all know I'm the number one target pagan of the week, too, don't they?"

We had learned not to argue with him.

Wally attempted a two-fisted hiking up of his pants, stuffing his shirttail in all around and then having to dig his suitcoat out of his belt. He buttoned it, leaving a swath of white shirt between the button and his belt and making a cursory yank at his tie as we stepped into the church.

He stiffened, as if on cue, and tried to walk a little taller and with more of a dignified bearing. He forgot to unbutton his coat until after we had sat down, however, and exhaled loudly after finally freeing his girth.

Wally would look on with us when hymns were sung, but he never sang. He recited the Lord's Prayer if it ever came up, and he always scrounged a few bills from his wallet when the plate was passed, though we had told him several times not to feel obligated. "If the people who show don't pay the bills, who's gonna?" was his logic.

There were many times when Margo and I would have felt more comfortable just putting the question to Wally. We fantasized about just asking him if there was any reason why he wouldn't want to believe in Christ and ask God to forgive his sin. That was a technique that had worked and was working for many people. But it hadn't seemed right with Earl and it didn't with Wally either. There were a ton of things he felt needed to be worked out first.

We knew better, of course. One of the beauties of faith in Christ is that He asks us to come as we are, with all our baggage, all our warts. We can't improve; we can't make ourselves better candidates, more presentable, more acceptable.

But try telling that to a man in his fifties who's spent his life in the pits of society, who's seen everything, who had four sons who "turned out bums," as he put it. One of them had just been released from jail, the ultimate humiliation for a cop.

Try telling it to a man who knows he has abused his body and his wife and his family for as long as he could remember. He and his wife had just started seeing each other again after having been married nearly thirty years and divorced for more than four. They had been miserable apart, and he had to see her occasionally, anyway, just for news about the boys and financial matters.

They had had dinner a few times, the old flames were rekindled some, and they were cautiously discussing a trial reconciliation. "I know she needs what you guys and Earl have, but who in the world am I to say that when I haven't got it myself and when I'm the reason she needs it so much?"

All we could do was look ahead to the day when God would work in Wally and make it clear to him how simple and uncomplicated the whole transaction would be. He was weighed down under the guilt of not having had time for his wife and his sons during their formative years, and as much as he tried to purge himself by calling them no-accounts and avoiding covering for them—as most parents would do—it was apparent that Wally felt he was to blame.

He had tried everything to become a tad straighter, to make himself more presentable. He had cleaned up his language to the point where gutter language only slipped out when he was mad and not as relish in normal conversation as was true with so many in his profession. And he had quit smoking.

"You wanna believe that's because I started seein' my wife again, but don't. That came from you and Margo and Earl and church and all that. I just wanted to do it. It hasn't hurt my appetite any, but I've kicked cigarettes, and I think it was because of all this."

We privately feared that his victory, and it was a big one after several decades of smoking, might get in his way. It went against everything we were trying to tell him. We wanted him to know that God would take him the way he was. And that God would help him with the things in his life that shouldn't be there. We had seen many people who became Christians and still suffered under the weight of personal habits for years. It was so important, we thought, that he see this simple point. And quitting smoking because of hanging around Christians and church made him think there was some mystical, magical benefit, but as wonderful as it was, it wasn't helping him see the larger, more important issue.

That morning in church, while the sermon was not on conversion, there were plenty of jumping off points for our discussion with Wally. We could have easily charged into our "is there any reason?" approach, but he had already made it clear—as Earl had so many times—that he didn't want to be pushed. He knew, he said, and when he was able to believe it, grasp it, understand it, see that it was as simple as we said it was, then maybe—

But not until then.

I had learned the hard way the danger of waiting until I thought someone was ready. But I had also learned that I can get in the way and do more harm than good if I don't back off sometimes and let God do His own work in His own time.

On the way back to our apartment I'm sure Margo had the same temptation I did, to just say, "So, Wally, how about it? You getting the drift? You ready? You wanna pray right now?"

And maybe he would have. He was covering well, pretending we hadn't just heard a sermon that had many discussable points for thinking adults. But Wally was like that. When things hit close to home, he would change the subject, pretending they hadn't reached him.

"Hey, I thought you were gonna let me take you out to dinner today!" he said as we passed one of his favorite haunts.

"Are you kidding?" Margo said. "All we ever do is eat out. Good grief, all *you* ever do is eat out. Here I am a newly married, traditional housewife type and you're not going to let me fix dinner?"

Wally held his hand over his heart and breathed a big sigh of relief. "Oh," he said, "for a minute there I thought you were saying that we ate out so much that we oughta skip lunch!" He moved up to the edge of the back seat and stared at me as I drove. I stole a glance at him.

"And how 'bout you, lover boy? You gonna let your wife do all the work?"

I started to respond, but Margo beat me to it. "As a matter of fact, he isn't. Philip enjoys preparing meals too, so some of what you'll eat this afternoon will be his work too."

"Oh no!" Wally said, clutching his throat and falling to the back of the seat again. I knew he'd be pleasantly surprised.

When Margo and I had a private moment before dinner, we agreed not to raise the issue of what we had heard at church unless he did. He was going to, but we didn't know because he started with business.

"So, where are you two on your innocent little friend?" he said with his mouth full, as usual.

"I'll tell you where I am," Margo responded without missing a beat. "I think you're wrong. I said so yesterday, and I haven't changed. If that girl is lying to us, she's the best con artist I've ever seen."

"Yeah, let me tell ya somethin', Margo Spence. Every time one of us in the profession gets hoodwinked by a sweet talkin' con artist, we protect ourselves, our image, you know what I mean, by sayin' this one was the best there ever was. I know from experience because I been taken by some of the best." He smiled knowingly. "You see what I mean? I think if they take me, they gotta be good."

"It's the truth," I said.

" 'Course it's the truth," Wally said, and Margo nodded. "I'm a good cop, huh? One of the best, right?" Somehow he had a way of saying it as a point-maker, so it didn't come off as bragging. We nodded again. It *was* true. "But I'm tellin' ya, I been taken and taken good. You see, it's the good ones who can swindle you so bad that you don't even know it's happened until they're out of town.

"I was hoodwinked by a gypsy one time who used the ruse that he was afraid of the gypsies because somebody said he looked like one. I bought it hook, line, and sinker. I musta spent half an hour convincing the guy that he didn't really look like a gypsy and that he didn't have to fear the gypsies because in the part of Chicago he was worried about, they just showed every year about that time and pulled a lot of petty stuff, two-bit short change jobs, small swindles, that type of thing.

"Thing is, he was so good at playing the innocent suburban blue collar thing that I felt sorry for him. In fact, it wasn't easy to convince him that there was no serious danger with the gypsies. He'd get up to leave and then come back and sit down and beg for more assurance that he had nothing to worry about."

"So, anyway, he was a con man?" Margo asked.

Wally paused dramatically and smiled at her. "He was only king of the gypsies," he said. "I busted him about ten days later, takin' downpayments on driveway sealant jobs, then never coming back to do the work."

"But Meaghan is so naive," Margo said.

"Who says so? Meaghan? Your problem is that you believe Meaghan about Meaghan. You see what I pulled out of her when I put the squeeze on?"

"Yes, but that just convinced me more that she's no hardened con artist. You really upset her with your probing."

"Did I? Or is she just good? They say the easiest lie to believe is the big one. She's a dope pusher, and she wants to sit there and have you believe that she wouldn't go to a party where people might be drinking or, horror of horrors, there might be mixed company?"

We couldn't keep from laughing. "I suppose she did sound too good to be true, Wally. But I want to believe her."

"That's it!" Wally said, nearly choking on his food. "She's got you. That's the game! When they can get you to want to believe them, you will. You'd love to think there's someone in the world who's that straight, and so you start buying it. Then, if she's consistent, which this one is—very good, actually—you're sucked in completely."

"But Wally, isn't it possible she's for real? I mean, what if she was?"

"If she's for real, it'll all come out in the wash. But you know what comes with that kinda logic."

"Yes, I know. If she's not, it'll come out too, especially with the infamous Wally Festschrift on the trail."

He grinned. "You're all right, Mrs. Spence, you know that?"

Margo smiled back. She did appreciate Wally. Even his rough edges. He stood briefly to push his chair back, then sat again and took a deep breath. "The last time I ate with a bunch of Christians, they served coffee after the meal and saved dessert until after the ballgame on TV. I hope that's not a religious ritual or anything, 'cause stuffed as I am and wonderful as all that was, ma'am—oh! and sir!—I always like to chase the meal with something sweet and heavy."

"Oh, I'm sorry, Wally," Margo deadpanned. "I hadn't planned on dessert today. Did you want me to run out and pick up something? I will."

"Oh, no, please," Wally said, actually blushing.

"No, I'll be happy to," she said. "A pie or something?"

"I'm sorry, honey," he said, "I was just teasing there. This was just great, and I just meant that if you *were* gonna have something, that I'd just as soon, you know, have it now instead of, you know, nah, I don't need anything really."

We burst out laughing. "You just got yourself taken by one of the best con artists in the business," I said.

Margo brought the dessert while Wally pressed his lips together and shook his head. "Yes," she said, "you've been wrong, I hope, for the second day in a row."

After his second piece of cake, which he pretended to have been coaxed into, Wally, still seated, put his hands on his hips and stared at Margo. "Delicious," he said. She nodded a thank-you. "I suppose you two are going to want to make this a weekly appointment."

"For Sunday dinner?" Margo said. "Sure."

"I s'pose I hafta come to church with you to qualify. I knew there'd be a catch."

Margo had started to protest, but it was apparent it was what Wally wanted, another reason to "have" to go to church with us against his will. "Well, fair enough then," he said, "I imagine the cake alone is worth the hassle."

"Nope," Margo said.

"Nope?" Wally repeated. "Nope what?"

"Nope, no cake unless you get up a little earlier and go with us to Sunday school too."

"You gotta be kiddin'! You guys still go to Sunday school? Whad'ya do, cut out stuff and listen to stories and all that?"

"No. We study the Bible or some Christian book and we discuss things."

He looked uncomfortable. "Will I hafta say anything?"

"Not unless you want to."

"I don't."

"Then you won't."

He appeared to be in thought. "Ah, cake's worth it," he said.

We watched some of the Cubs game on television before Wally left, and Margo mentioned that she bet that was what Meaghan was doing right then, too.

"You even bought the sports and country music fan bit, huh?" Wally said.

"You don't believe *anything* she said?" Margo asked.

Wally paused. "No, can't say that I do. And we'll see how much *you* believe after tomorrow morning's assignment meeting. I've got a surprise for you. For both of you."

Chapter Seven

Of course I had seen Jules Perkins precisely forty-eight hours before he appeared at the door of the EH Detective Agency the next morning. Yet I wouldn't have recognized him, except for the deformed fingernail Meaghan had pointed out. But then, I hadn't seen the fingernail on Saturday. Had Mr. Perkins seen me?

He shook my hand slowly and stared deep into my eyes, much as he had done so quickly at the parking garage elevators at O'Hare. He nodded and his eyes shifted to Wally while his face remained turned toward mine.

"I wondered," he said in a voice so soft it startled me. He would prove precise, articulate, deliberate. "But I merely filed your face away in my mind. Had I seen you again that day, I'd have certainly put it together. Tell me something, were you also the driver of the blue Skylark?"

"Yes, sir," I said, impressed. There had been no indication that my "priest" had been aware of being followed.

"And you were likely the passenger," he said to Margo, "sitting close to the driver, pretending to be a lover or girlfriend or new wife or something."

Wally guffawed, and Jules Perkins got a kick out

of the fact that his not-so-professional trailers were indeed newlyweds. "Now then, Sergeant Festschrift, I assume you're going to tell me how your firm was put onto the Meaghan Hanekamp case and by whom."

We assembled in Earl Haymeyer's old office, where Wally had placed a table and several cheap metal folding chairs. Perkins carefully laid his folded-over jacket on the table and sat down, crossing his legs and pulling a small notebook and pen from his shirt pocket.

Wally had the Hanekamp file in his hand, and when he didn't immediately open it, Perkins reminded him that he didn't have much time. "I am assigned to tail this woman constantly," he said. "She has a flight this afternoon."

"Yes, and we have promised her that one of us would be on it with her so she wouldn't have to fear you so much."

Perkins squinted at Wally, unmoving. Wally returned the stare. I had assumed Mr. Perkins was unflappable, but he didn't appear so now. "What are you saying, Sergeant?"

"You heard it," Wally said, not unkindly. "We told Meaghan Hanekamp—"

"You have been in direct contact with the suspect?"

"Of course."

"And this is not a problem with your client?"

"Our client?"

Perkins was annoyed. "Your client, your client, whoever tipped you off about Hanekamp and wanted her followed. I've been following her for about three months."

"She's been onto you for about two," Wally said carefully.

If Perkins could have looked startled, he did. "She told you this?"

Wally nodded. 'The pinkie nail gave you away, Jules."

He looked at his hand and swore. "If she's onto me, she's better than I thought."

"C'mon," Wally said. "You oughta know better'n to try to go without covering that finger."

"I'm not talking about her making me," Perkins said. "I'm talking about her sheer ability as a con."

I sneaked a peek at Margo. She appeared stunned.

"She's given me nothing to indicate that she knew. She's a pro, just as we suspected. But still, Festschrift, who are you working for?"

"You don't see it yet?"

Perkins swore. "You always were a game-player, Festschrift. Just get on with it."

"Our client," Wally said slowly, almost as if mimicking Perkins, "is Meaghan Hanekamp."

Perkins pursed his lips and stared, comprehending but not liking what he heard. "So now you're going to tell me that a federal felony suspect is your client and that you've been following me ever since she made me two months ago? Give me more credit than that. You think I don't check out the whole plane every time I get the chance? I'm banking on the fact that this guy here [he pointed at me] was on a flight with Hanekamp and me for the first time Saturday, am I right? Otherwise, what disguises has he been using?"

"You're right, Jules," Wally said. "She's been

onto you for two months; we've only been onto you for two days."

Perkins was, by now, clearly irritated. "So what're you going to do, Wally? You knew when you found out it was me that this was a federal drug case, so you've got to back off. Can I assume you're backing off?"

"Will that help?"

"You won't be of any help any other way. We don't want anyone in the way; we don't want anyone getting hurt; and we don't need a good detective agency working for the other side. Somebody's gonna wind up dead."

"We're a good detective agency?"

Perkins smiled a wry grin. "That's what they said when Earl Haymeyer ran it."

"Oh, you're cute," Wally said. "I've got half a mind to stay on this case and hound you for my client, making sure you do everything right. If you don't we'll give her what she needs to beat the rap."

Perkins's smile froze. "Obstruction of federal justice is a serious offense, Wally. You know that."

"I know that, and you don't really think I'd take the side of a drug pusher, do you? 'Pete's sake, Jules, you guys who get to the fed level got pigeon brains or what?"

"So you're going to back off?"

"Not until I know you've got something solid on her."

"I can't tell you anything, Wally."

"And I don't have to back off. I have a bona fide client here. Why should I let her hang out to dry?"

"Because you know they wouldn't have me on the

case unless we were putting together something big."

"Yeah, well, great, let's start tellin' each other how good we are, OK? How come you think this gal's employing us, huh? Because I know you from way back? Wise up, Jules. Your boys put you on it 'cause you're good. Miss Hanekamp wants us on it because she's afraid of you—and because we're good. So we're not backin' off until we know what you got. I wouldn't be able to sleep at night if I let you bust an innocent girl, especially a client of mine."

"Oh, Sergeant Festschrift, my heart bleeds," Perkins said, and it was then that I sensed some of the depth of the steel that made up his core. He was tough and mean and afraid of nothing. And now he sat there in silence. Wally tried a different tack.

"So what'd you think when you saw the blue Skylark followin' you to Chicago?"

"What'd I think? I thought it was one of the crowd Meaghan Hanekamp's been running with, but with a new car. I ran a ten-twenty-eight on the plate. It registered to a Spence and the Spence worked for EH, and so when you called, I figured something was up, like double coverage, like maybe one of the state or local agencies or say perhaps the Illinois Department of Law Enforcement was interested in the case. You don't know anybody there, do you?"

Nobody except Earl Haymeyer, who had recently left us to become head of the IDLE.

"So you still haven't told us what you've got, and until I get that, I can't even think about backing off. What if I told you that at this point, our client is totally, and I mean totally, unaware of why you're following her? She maintains she's straight, doesn't smoke, drink, or chew, or go with guys who do."

Perkins smiled.

"I'm also tellin' ya, Jules, more'n half our staff believes her."

Perkins was squinting again. He looked around the room. "Uh-huh, tell me another one. Tell me that you're in the believing half, Wally. Go ahead."

It was a deft move by a pro. Not many can slow Wally when he's on a roll. He only hesitated a moment. "The only thing that means anything is that she's a client, signed, sealed, and delivered, and one of us is going to be on that plane with you this afternoon, Jules. Got any more information, or are you going to make this difficult for all of us?"

"Wally, you're an old friend; why make this difficult for yourself? It's not going to hurt me any. All I need to do is to get an injunction against you."

"From a federal judge? And you don't call that trouble for *you?* Think of what you gotta go through for that. And how you gonna explain it? 'Well, yer honor, sir, these small time local private detectives are in the middle of our big bad federal investigation and they keep gettin' in our way. Make 'em stop, please!' "

Perkins was not amused. "Give me a break, Wally. What is this?"

"C'mon, Jules! What's a little info gonna cost ya? I won't hurt you with it, I promise. Gimme enough to satisfy me that we shouldn't work for this girl. Something good enough that I'll be on your side for no charge. How 'bout it?"

The slight, dark-haired man stared at Wally and

then out the window. "What do you want to know?" he asked finally.

"Just a little somethin' from your notebook there, Jules. Just a little of anything solid you've got on the girl, something that will convince the skeptics among us." He winked at Margo.

Perkins stood and paced, leafing through his little notepad. His feet stopped when his finger did. "How about something very recent and very big? Will that do?"

"Sure."

"On Sunday, May first in Los Angeles, she accepted six thousand dollars in a nine-by-twelve manila envelope in exchange for several ounces of cocaine, delivered in a small flight bag."

Margo gasped, almost inaudibly. "How do you know that?" she asked.

"I witnessed the transaction, Mrs. Spence. The buy was made from one of our agents, a female in L.A. Need anything else, Wally?"

"You've given me that; give me a couple more. Anything more recent?"

"Uh, yeah. Five days later she accepted a cashier's check for fifteen hundred dollars from an informant to our Boston bureau and gave him a key and a note telling him where he would find a quantity of contraband prescription drugs. The key fit a luggage locker at Logan where we confiscated several hundred hallucinogens and downers."

"Anything else?" Wally asked, sounding disappointed, though he was only having his own suspicions confirmed. "We might as well hear it all."

"Let me say this: in the three months I've been tracking her, Miss Hanekamp has made illegal drug transactions totaling more than thirty thousand dollars. All but the Boston drop involved cash, and only one was bizarre. That was the one I was involved in."

"You made a transaction with her, Jules?" Wally asked.

"And what was bizarre about it?" Margo added.

"Early on, about the fourth time I flew with her, I posed as a middle-aged woman and purchased a number ten envelope from her for about eight thousand dollars. What was bizarre wasn't the fact that I was dressed as a woman, but the way in which the dope was transmitted. Inside the envelope was one sheet of high quality, high rag content, stationery. It was a bleached white parchment-type with no letterhead, just the watermark of one of the fancy paper companies."

"That's *it?*" I said. "You paid all that money and she stuck you with a nice piece of paper? She was onto you or what?"

"Not at all. Invisible to the naked eye, but detectable under infra-red light, was a pattern of tiny discs, in diameter about the size of aspirins. Chemically treated and removed from the paper, they proved to be concentrated tabs of lysergic acid diethylamide. Acid. LSD."

Margo stood and moved to the window. Perkins sat back down. "She's got a lot of connections," he said. "That younger brother of hers, a college dropout, is a real head. Buys, sells, holds, uses, you name it. She's not a user, far as we can tell. Stays pretty clean. She'll have to be caught in the act; she's not the type you'll pick up in a big bust of any sort. She's not the party type."

"She told us that," Margo said, "among other things."

We were all depressed. Even Perkins hadn't seemed to enjoy the account. Of course, Wally had had to drag it out of him as it was. We moseyed out into the outer office and looked everywhere but into each other's eyes.

"No one knows you're on this case but me," Perkins said. "So, just quietly drop out, and that will be the end of it. You won't have to have anyone know that you had a client who wound up in federal prison or dead, either one."

"We can't drop out," Wally said flatly.

Perkins swore again. "What *are* you talking about, Festschrift? You want to get us both in bad trouble and get somebody hurt, don't you?"

"I'm only thinking of you, Jules. If we drop out now, Meaghan has to know why. What are we supposed to tell her?"

Wally knew he had Perkins. The latter stood with his hands deep in his pockets. "What are you suggesting, Wally?"

"Let us help you. We won't get paid, but we'd like to see dope pushers out of business as much as you would."

"I can't let you help, Wally. It's bigger than this Hanekamp woman. It's the whole crew, most of it anyway. This Dwayne makes most of the drops. Carole has made several, but she and Dwayne are a little more visible. They've been busted before, never convicted. We've been watching them for a long time, hoping for a break. We've seen enough so that we're ready for a good bust, but we have to take them all at once."

"Can't we help in some way, Jules?"

"There's no way, Wally. You know we can't inter-mix agencies, especially private and governmental. I mean, you never mixed municipal with private, did you?" Wally stared at him, unsmiling. And Perkins remembered. Wally was currently under investigation and up for possible suspension of all his pension benefits because of having helped EH in a murder case before he had resigned from the Chicago Police Department. "Oh, I'm sorry, Wally. I wasn't thinking. But there, you see? You don't want that to happen to me, do you? I couldn't do it without permission, and there's no way I could get permission before today's flight. Anyway, they'd never allow it. I'm not the only one they've got on this case; you know that. I'm not even the only one who's been on the planes with the suspects, though I'm the only one who's been on every one of Hanekamp's flights. What do you want to do this for, Wally? You're asking for trouble."

"We don't like bein' duped anymore'n the next guy. Am I right, kids?" he said, looking at us. "Wouldn't you like to be involved in this, seeing her get what she deserves?"

I nodded. Margo was more cautious. "But Mr. Perkins has a point, Wally. This isn't our case. We have no jurisdiction. We'd just be in the way. I don't know what we're going to tell Meaghan, though. How do we handle that, Mr. Perkins? We did promise her we'd be on the plane this afternoon."

He looked at his watch and put his coat on. "Let me tell you this much more," he said. "If you can just beg off from today's flight for some reason, you may not have to worry about what to say to her in the future."

Wally couldn't let *that* go without explanation. "Something's goin' down today, Jules?"

"Very possibly. That's all I can say, Wally, so please don't ask anything more."

"I'm not promising anything," Wally said, as Perkins headed for the door. He turned back, annoyed.

"What!" he demanded.

"Jules," Wally said, trying to be soothing. "I heard everything you said, so it won't be your fault if we're there."

"You want me to bring you up on charges? Something happens there today because you guys are in the way, and I'll tell them I ordered you to stay away."

"You can't order anything without a judge," Wally said, "and I've never known a mortal who can keep me or one of my people from the scene of some action."

"See?" Perkins said, angry now. "I can't trust you with information. I shouldn't have told you anything. You do what you have to do, and I'll do what I have to do."

"You do that, Julie. And remember I love ya, no matter what happens. Who knows? Maybe havin' one of my people out there today will be one of the best things that ever happened to you."

"Yeah, sure! Anybody ever tell you you're a lousy guy, Festschrift?" he said as he opened the door.

"A lotta guys," Wally said, moving toward the ringing phone. "But none so classy as you."

With a dirty look, Jules Perkins was gone, and Wally answered the phone. "Hello, EH, this is Festschrift. . . .Oh, just a minute, honey, I gotta put you on hold a second. Hang on."

"It's her!" Wally said, mashing the hold button. "Get Perkins back here."

Margo skipped out the door and down the stairs, returning with the still boiling but now intrigued federal narcotics agent. "Everybody get on a phone," Wally instructed. "And unscrew the mouthpiece, fast! C'mon, I can't stall her forever. Everybody set? Punch in on line two and watch me. When I pick up, we all pick up. Ready? OK."

We all lifted our receivers at the same time so it would make one sound in her ear. "I'm sorry, Meaghan, but I had somebody here. Go ahead."

"I wanted to tell you how glad I am that someone from your office will be on the flight with me today, and I was wondering who it was going to be and whether they would stay with me for the whole thing."

"What's the whole thing, Meaghan?"

"It's an L.A. to Chicago to Boston and the same way back. I'm picking it up on the second leg here from Chicago to Boston. I know that guy will be on it all the way too, because he always seems to know when I'm flying."

"I don't know," Wally said. "We haven't actually decided yet who should go. Maybe we'll have one go with you from Chicago to Boston and back, and then someone else from Chicago to L.A. and back."

"That would be fine, Mr. Festschrift, but hadn't you better settle it soon? You'll need to get tickets pretty quickly."

Perkins was giving Wally a threatening look, waving at him, as if telling him to get out of going somehow. Wally wasn't getting the message, so Perkins wrote on a sheet of paper: "At least get out of the first round trip leg."

"Uh, listen, Meaghan, I wonder if it would be OK if I sent Philip on that Chicago to L.A. round trip with you."

"Sure. And who would be on the Chicago-Boston run?"

"Ah, yeah, well maybe no one. We're awfully busy around here today, and I imagine that flight will be hard to get on by now."

Meaghan was silent for a moment. "Is that your final word?" she asked.

"Yeah, I'm afraid it will have to be. I'm sorry."

"I don't like it much. We had a deal."

"I know. I'm sorry."

Suddenly she brightened. "Well, hey, maybe it'll save me some money. I pay for these flights, don't I?"

"Yeah, that's true enough."

"Well, now I have to come up with an excuse for me."

"Pardon me?"

"I told you I wouldn't go alone. If you can't arrange for someone to go with me, I'm not going. Maybe I can come up with an emergency that will keep me from getting to the eastbound plane to Boston, but that will allow me to pick it up before the L.A. run."

Perkins looked panicky, as if that would be the worst possible solution. He looked as if he thought having one of us go, thus forcing her to go, would be better than the alternative. Wally noticed, and likely assumed, as I did, that there was definitely going to be some action. "Uh, OK, listen, Meaghan, I think I can spring Philip here pretty soon. We don't want you to jeopardize your job with another disciplinary problem."

"You're right, that could have been a problem with all the trouble I've been in lately. Oh, thank you so much. This is such a relief because I saw him today."

"You saw who today?"

"The guy who's been following me, of course."

"You saw him where?"

"From my apartment window. He hung around my building for an hour or so. Left about twenty minutes ago."

Chapter Eight

So now what was Meaghan up to? The Federal Narcotics Bureau couldn't have a major bust in the works unless they knew a major transaction was in the works. Jules Perkins thought it strange that Meaghan actually threatened not to fly to Boston without one of us on the plane. That told me he was expecting something big and that he apparently thought Meaghan would be using us as an alibi in some way. Before he left the office, he told me, "You're only going so we can be sure *she's* going, so don't get any ideas. Stay away from me, don't try to follow me or talk to me or anything. Just stay out of it."

I looked to Wally. He nodded. So I nodded too.

What I hadn't bargained for was how quickly Meaghan had returned to the good graces of her superiors. I mean, how was I supposed to know she would be back in first class again already? Jules knew, of course. He had connections I didn't have, and Meaghan either didn't know in time or didn't want me to know.

During the flight to Boston, while I was stuck back in the coach smoking section, Jules was in first class but not in disguise. I couldn't figure that for beans. Now that he knew she was onto him, why wouldn't he want to make her think the pressure was off?

Especially if they were assuming something big was coming down tonight.

I don't know. Maybe he wanted her to think that he thought the sale would happen in Boston. Maybe she really hadn't connected her follower to her drug business yet. *Yeah, and I'm the Easter bunny,* I thought.

Midway through the flight, Meaghan found a reason to walk to the back of the plane. On her way back up, she dropped me a note.

"Stay close. He's here in first class. I'm not getting off in Boston. He probably won't, either. I'm going to run a quick errand when we get back to Chicago, but unless he follows me, you don't need to get off either."

How naive did this woman think I was? A quick errand in Chicago? And maybe he wouldn't follow her? Craziness. But the real shock came when Perkins deplaned in Boston. I couldn't imagine why he was letting her out of his sight. Now would she get off too? No, she didn't. Should I get off and try to make contact with him to see what was going on? I was tempted, but I didn't. He had made my instructions clear.

Baffling to both of us, Perkins did not seem to reboard for the flight to Chicago. For the first hour, Meaghan made periodic trips up and down the aisles, apparently not believing her eyes. Finally she stopped at my seat, and pretending to ask if I needed anything, whispered, "I think he's actually not on the plane, but I can't be sure. If he's not, it's the first time in months."

That made me wonder if he hadn't outdone himself with a new name and disguise and seat reservation. I looked around too. Was he the old man in the back? The old woman in the front? He could have been anyone.

The next time Meaghan came around, I asked her if she was sure she didn't need me to keep an eye on her in Chicago. "I'm so relieved he's not here. No, I'll be all right. I'm only going to be off the plane for a few minutes. In fact, if I can be sure he's not on the plane to L.A., I can probably get you off right before takeoff. There's no sense wasting your time if he's not going to be bothering me."

"But what if he's waiting for you in L.A.?"

"I never thought of that. I guess you'd better come, regardless. If you don't mind."

"I don't mind," I said, wondering how I'd feel if I saw her get busted right before my eyes. When she headed back to first class, I was overwhelmed with pity for her. I had felt similarly when I thought she was being followed on every flight. Now that I knew the truth about her *and* her follower, I was moved just as much.

I prayed silently that God would somehow work in her life. She ran in fast circles and played a dangerous game. Maybe she was beyond any feeling of a need for God, and yet, who ever really knows? Maybe she was tired of the life already. Maybe the lies and the phoniness and the danger had already caught up with her. Maybe she was ripe for a big change. I prayed that she was, and that if Margo or I could be used in any way, whether now or even after whatever was going to happen to her, God would give us the wisdom to say or do whatever was necessary.

By the time we touched down in Chicago, I

realized that I had just spent more hours away from Margo than I had since we'd been married. I missed her, thought about her, and wished I didn't have to go to California. We were held so long on the ground in Chicago that the captain came on to tell us that we would be rescheduled for a slightly later departure, giving us forty minutes from the time we reached the gate. I had time to get off and call Margo.

"You're not going to recognize this place when you get back tomorrow," she said. "I'm making it totally livable."

"I wouldn't recognize a totally livable apartment?" I asked, trying to sound wounded.

"Not one intended for a married couple to live in, no," she said. "You'll like it. And if you don't, we can change it. I got all our wedding presents unpacked and the boxes and trash thrown away. I got all my stuff out and arranged. I did a little rearranging of furniture too. I just thought you'd be happy if I got it all done and you didn't have to worry about it."

"That was sweet, and I can't wait to—"

"What is it, Philip?"

I whispered, "Meaghan just went by, a little earlier than I expected. She's not carrying anything but her over-sized purse. You can tell Wally that Perkins was not on the flight back from Boston. I don't know what he's up to, but it wouldn't surprise me to see him in L.A."

"It wouldn't surprise *me* if you saw him in Chicago. Are you going to follow her?"

"Nah, I don't think so—oh, Margo! You're right! It's Perkins! He stepped out of one of those little bars between the gates. I don't know whether to follow him or not. Whatever's gonna happen is gonna happen tonight."

"Follow him, Philip! You'll regret it if you don't."

"You're right. I'll see ya. Love you."

"Love you. Bye. Be careful."

I jogged to cut the distance between myself and Perkins. He was about fifty feet behind Meaghan, who was moving fairly quickly. I was shocked to see Perkins turn a complete circle at one point, as if to be sure he wasn't being followed. I happened to be moving in behind three servicemen at the time and was just out of his sight as he whirled. Was he looking for me? Who else? Maybe his partners? Should I try to elude him?

Meaghan was increasing her lead, so Perkins trotted a few steps and then settled into a faster pace. I did the same, but it left me exposed and vulnerable the next time he spun around to check both flanks. And he saw me.

I tried to slow up and appear harmless, but he quickly turned back, glaring at me, running backwards now, not losing any ground on his prey. He scowled and pointed directly at me and gestured that I should stop. I stopped. He turned around again, and I started up again.

One thing I knew for sure: I didn't want him to see me again. I didn't know if what I was doing was illegal. I didn't know if I was disobeying an order from a federal marshal or what. I couldn't say I didn't understand what he wanted. He wanted me to stop following him.

When he wasn't looking back, I sprinted up as far as I dared and ducked into a waiting area or a gate. Then I'd peer out and watch him wheel around.

When I thought it was safe, I'd dash out again, once almost coming within ten feet of him before slipping into one of the stand-up phone booths as he was turning again.

Finally, I think he was satisfied that I had given up, and he quit looking. Meanwhile, he had picked up about ten feet on Meaghan, who had not once turned to see if she had been followed. Either she was confident he was still in Boston, or she simply had her mind on her "errand."

We were nearing the Y where two concourses merged before leading to the ticket counters and baggage claim areas. Perkins slowed perceptibly, and I sensed he might take one more look back. I scooted into a tiny fast food counter just as he turned. He turned back just in time to see Meaghan turn right into the next concourse.

Perkins, a smart but cautious federal agent, didn't immediately follow. Without causing a scene, he moved to his right against the wall, cut through a short open area, and wound up pressed behind a beam, a vantage point from which he could see Meaghan for a long way without being immediately behind her.

I stopped too, but I wasn't as hidden from Perkins as I would have liked. He was intent on watching Meaghan now, though, and I was convinced, as I think he was, that she was unaware of him. He leaned far around the beam as she continued to move farther from him, and it soon became apparent that he would have to move too. But moving into the concourse corridor would expose him if she chose to turn around. There weren't nearly as many people as there had been in the busier concourse, and except for one bank of phones, there was nowhere to duck into and hide if necessary.

Still, Perkins felt it necessary to follow. And as he moved out, he reached into his coat and pulled out a tiny walkie-talkie microphone and whispered into it. It may have been my imagination, but several medium-sized men in conservative dress seemed to materialize from various points, some coming from the concourse we'd been on, and others appearing from the main ticketing area.

It doesn't take a sixth sense to realize that men who have bulges in their hip pockets and carry no luggage are at the airport for more than sightseeing. When I finally edged into the concourse myself, knowing full well now that Perkins would eventually see me and chew me out, I was able to slow down and survey the situation.

There weren't many men now that I could say for certain were with Perkins. Maybe only one other. Had the rest been my imagination working overtime? My biggest conviction now was that Meaghan definitely had no idea she was being followed. No one who was afraid of being followed would venture down a dead-end corridor. To get out of this place, which she knew well, she would have to go back *toward* Perkins and whoever was with him.

Whether Perkins knew *he* was still being followed, I didn't know. And how he got here I didn't know either. Had he fooled us both with an incredible disguise, or had he taken a fast flight back to Chicago before we had even left the ground in Boston?

I was so excited, and so lost in thought, that I nearly missed it when Perkins stopped and pressed up against the wall. Luckily, he was looking only ahead at Meaghan, because he could have seen me not far behind him. I stopped, virtually in the middle of the corridor and watched as Meaghan warmly greeted a middle-aged woman, not as if she had known her before, but—again, I was guessing—as if they had just met and Meaghan was very glad about it.

Meaghan looked at her watch, appeared to be apologizing, and then reached into her bag and traded envelopes with the woman. As soon as the transaction was made, Perkins approached the pair, his hand inside his coat, resting, I assumed, on his weapon.

When he was within about thirty feet of them the older woman looked him full in the face. When he nodded to her, she dropped quickly to all fours, startling Meaghan and causing her to peer up the hallway at Perkins.

She looked genuinely puzzled, and horrified, as if she couldn't make it compute—this woman she apparently had just met dropping to the floor and her stalker of at least two months moving toward her with his hand menacingly in his coat. She froze.

Suddenly, I thought I heard the tell-tale *chink-chink* of a high-powered pistol with a silencer firing two quick shots. Perkins reeled backward, his head smacking the marble-like floor first, blood gushing from his chest and face. Nearly catatonic, I moved numbly toward him, vaguely aware that Meaghan's handbag and the pistol slid across the floor and stopped at the wall.

The woman on the floor moaned and covered her head with her hands, and I thought I saw a figure run from behind an otherwise empty boarding area toward what should have been a locked gate door. Meaghan had flown past me, screaming a name that would only come to me later, cutting between two men with guns drawn who ignored her and ran, one to Perkins and one to the woman. She appeared only scared. Perkins, however, was unmistakably dead—with eyes open and teeth bared.

I started toward the gun, my legs rubbery, and the man who had bent over the woman helped her to her feet and waved his gun at me. "Don't touch it," he ordered. "Leave it where it lies!"

Before I could think, I took off running after Meaghan. A crowd had already begun to form; people were screaming and gasping. Police were coming from every direction. I raced through the concourse to the Y and looked both ways. Meaghan had headed out, toward the ticket counters. It was a busy Monday night, and she was having trouble fighting through the crowd. I figured I could take advantage of the path she was clearing. What I would do with her if I caught up with her, I didn't know.

Running at top speed and zigzagging between clusters of curious, milling people who wondered where we were going, I closed the gap on Meaghan until I thought I would be able to catch her within ten or fifteen more strides. But when she broke into the clear into an open area several hundred feet long, she ran so fast I was shocked.

Fortunately for her, she was wearing culottes and had rubber-soled shoes. Unencumbered by any weight, and very obviously an experienced, trained runner, she lowered her head, lifted her knees, pumped her arms in a furious rhythm to match her legs, and left me far behind.

Emotion began to well up in me as the image of Perkins worked on my brain. I settled into the fastest long-distance pace I could handle—which was faster than normal due to the adrenalin—and decided I would simply outlast Meaghan. With her handbag on the floor near a dead man, she wasn't going anywhere.

I had never seen a woman run so fast or so efficiently. Was it only the terror? She had to have run in competition. I hadn't seen a gun in her hand, but one had certainly slid away from her along with her bag. And what was it she had screamed on her way past me?

Would she try for a cab? She had no money. Maybe she'd promise some money when she reached her apartment, but how would she get in? She needed her key. How long could she maintain this pace? She continued driving through the hallways at an incredible rate, forcing people to jump clear.

As she came to the ticket counter area, a slow thinking lobbyist for somebody or other stepped in front of her with his placard and petition. There was no time to slow down, so she stiff-armed him onto his seat and he slid back almost twenty feet. She had to dance to keep her feet, and I gained a little on her, but my chest was heaving and my mouth was dry. I ached all over and still fought the awful memory of Perkins on the ground.

Meaghan bullied her .way past the crowd on the down escalator, and the bottleneck allowed me to come within range again. I caught a glimpse of the terror on her face, but she showed no sign of fatigue. That was not encouraging. I worried she would find another open stretch and leave me as if I were stopped. Where did she think she was going?

My fear was realized. As Meaghan skipped down the steps to the lower level leading to the parking garage elevators, similar to where I had followed Perkins following her three days before, she ignored the automated pedestrian tram and sped up again. I could only hope I'd catch her at the elevators.

But when she got there, she didn't want to wait for a car. The door to the stairs was closing as I arrived. I was almost too weak to open it, and I dreaded even the thought of chasing this fleet young woman up a flight of stairs, or several flights.

When I got the door opened, she was halfway up the first flight, and her pace had finally caught up with her. She stumbled and tumbled to her knees, trying to climb but unable to make any progress with her spent leg muscles. I gripped the rail hard and pulled myself slowly up to her. She was sobbing, but she heard me and peeked out from behind her hands.

"Oh! Mr. Spence! Oh, I can't believe it! I hoped and prayed you had followed me, but I didn't think you had." She broke down and embraced me, crying loudly. "Oh, he's dead! He's dead! Did you see him? Who *was* he, anyway? Was he trying to kill me? Dwayne saved me, and I didn't even know Dwayne was there! That woman, she acted like she knew him, almost like she was setting me up for him, but she couldn't have been. That was Carole's aunt!"

It was starting to make sense to me, but I couldn't be sure about her. Was she still conning me, or was it possible she had been as naive as she seemed all along? Could someone be used in such a complicated scheme and not know it? I wanted to believe that, because I had been impressed by Meaghan's personality from the start—at least what *appeared* to be her personality.

"Where're you going, Meaghan?" I asked, hardly able yet to catch my breath.

"To my car. I've got a key hidden under the bumper. We should get out of here, shouldn't we?"

"I suppose we should, but we'd better take my car. They could already be watching for yours by the time you get out of the garage." The truth was, I *knew* the Federal Narcotics Bureau boys were aware of her car, her apartment, everything.

We staggered up the stairs to the third level, where I had parked. "What happened back there, anyway, Meaghan?"

"I don't know. I was only delivering a message for Carole because she didn't have time to get off the plane, and all of a sudden there was the guy who had been following me all this time. I saw him when Carole's aunt fell, and he looked like he was going to kill me. I didn't even have time to scream when someone shot him, shot him right there, and tossed away the gun."

"Meaghan," I said, a chill going through me, "who tossed you the gun?"

"It was Dwayne. It *looked* like Dwayne. I was so scared, I don't know *what* happened.

I slid behind the wheel and pulled out, noticing a lot of action in the rearview mirror, police and security guards pouring from the elevators. "Take your cap and jacket off, quick," I said. "The ticket-takers are going to be looking for a flight attendant."

She was soon sitting there in her culottes and a white blouse. "Maybe you'd better pretend you're asleep," I suggested. "In case one of these people in the booths might recognize you." She laid her head back and faced the door, sighing heavily and shuddering. For an instant, I wished I could break down and cry.

Chapter Nine

I put my hand on her elbow. "I need to ask you one more thing, Meaghan. Did you touch the gun?"

"Yes," she said quickly. "I caught it with both hands, and that made my bag slip off my shoulder. And when I flung the gun away, I lost my bag too."

I groaned. We were in big, big trouble. I started looking for a phone booth. I needed Wally and Margo at the office when we arrived for this one. I didn't want to be harboring a murder suspect all by myself.

I decided not to risk being seen at a phone booth too close to the airport, so I planned a route that would take me all the way downtown, then back up north via the Edens. Then I would get off at Touhy, heading east to Ridge, which I would take north to Green Bay Road up to Glencoe. Somewhere along that path, I would stop and call Wally and Margo.

As soon as I had paid the parking bill and we moved into the traffic toward the city, Meaghan sat up and buried her face in her hands. She cried and cried. I didn't know what to think. Was it possible she still didn't know what had happened?

I turned on the radio and found WBBM AM at 780, an all-news station. As a commercial ended, the newsman reported: "Details are sketchy at this moment, but a major crime story is breaking at O'Hare International Airport where a TransCoastal

Airlines flight attendant, Meaghan Hanekamp, twenty-six, is being sought in the fatal shooting of a Federal Narcotics Bureau agent, 44-year-old Jules Perkins, formerly of Chicago, currently of Washington, D.C.

"Police say the shooting took place within the last several minutes and that Miss Hanekamp, a suspected illegal drug dealer, fled on foot, possibly with an accomplice.

"Police say Miss Hanekamp fired upon the agent from close range, apparently when he approached after she had sold a controlled substance to an undercover female federal narcotics agent. The female agent, who has not been identified, is reported unhurt."

Meaghan sat silent and motionless with her fingers pressed against her temples, staring wide-eyed at the radio, her mouth open, as if about to scream. If I'd had to stake my life on it, I'd bet she was totally, genuinely mortified. She turned to me, as if to speak, her hands still pressed to the sides of her head, but more news came from the radio.

"Our Larry Crawford happened to be at O'Hare this evening on a feature assignment, and we have him on the line right now. Yes, Larry, what can you tell us about what's happening out there now?"

"Right, uh, Bill, it's nothing but mass confusion here now as police and federal authorities believe that the uh, stewardess, Meaghan Hanekamp, may still be in the complex. Dozens of witnesses have told authorities that the woman, still in her TransCoastal Airlines uniform, was seen running from the scene of the slaying.

"At this moment, she has been reported seen as

far away from the scene as the pedestrian tram leading to the parking garage elevators, however authorities doubt the accuracy of those reports because they have determined that she would likely have had to run as far as a quarter of a mile, through heavy foot traffic here, in less than a minute. Highly unlikely."

"Indeed, Larry. Can you tell us, if you know, was this some sort of a major operation by the federal authorities?"

"Yes, as far as I can tell. The federal people here, from the narcotics bureau, are not saying much, but a Chicago police officer and a security guard at the airport both told me they understood that this was the first arrest in a series of arrests that would have broken up a small but wide-ranging operation that included several airline employees."

Meaghan screeched, "Philip! What are they *talking* about? We have to go back! I was running an errand, and the man who has been following me got shot! *I* didn't shoot him! I think Dwayne did! Turn around! We have to go back and tell them!"

I held up a hand to silence her so I could hear the radio.

"Bill, I've been able to talk with a federal agent here who refuses to talk on the air, but he tells me that the suspect dropped at the scene of the crime both her handbag and the high-powered handgun used to kill Jules Perkins.

"A massive search of the entire complex is taking place at this time, mainly concentrating on the route where Miss Hanekamp was reported last seen running on foot. A major traffic snarl is already building from the parking garages to the ticket booths as police search every car on its way out.

"All flights from gates in Concourse D have been canceled or assigned to other gates, so passengers on Eastern, Delta, and some United flights should call the airport before leaving home."

"Larry, do you have any more on exactly what took place before the shooting?"

"Yes, Bill. It seems the Federal Narcotics Bureau had several similar arrests planned for this evening, but none involving actual drug and cash transactions. This was the first, and the others were to follow within the hour."

"Is it safe to say, Larry, that this tragic incident has aborted the rest of the operation?"

"That's the case, Bill. Apparently the authorities needed this first arrest to pave the way for the others, but that is only speculation, and I didn't get that totally from the federal authorities here."

"Are you in a position to tell us if and when the, ah, suspect, Miss, uh—"

"Hanekamp, Meaghan Hanekamp."

"Right. When she is located there?"

"I am, Bill, however, most authorities here are pessimistic about the chances of finding her the longer the search goes on."

"And what about the other arrests, should she be located?"

"I'm only guessing again, Bill, but I imagine the publicity surrounding her arrest, if it came now, has already made the subsequent arrests impossible. Excuse me, Bill, here's an interesting note from my assistant here. It seems that some members of flight crews on various planes from different airlines out here are refusing to deplane at the request of federal agents, claiming international immunity while aboard the aircraft. That doesn't necessarily mean they are under investigation, of course, but it seems that those who have heard about the incident and don't want to be involved are invoking this unusual privilege. Whether they can actually get away with it without repercussion, we'll have to see. No doubt such action will prove embarrassing to their respective employers."

"Thank you, Larry. And we'll be returning to O'Hare whenever anything breaks in this tragic case. Repeating, a federal narcotics agent has been shot to death, apparently by a flight attendant . . ."

Meaghan appeared as if she were going to be sick. "Are you all right?" I asked.

"Am I all right? That man was murdered and they think I did it! No, I'm not all right! And what is that all about, all that drug business and narcotics bureau?"

"You really still don't know?"

"What do you mean? No!"

"You haven't been selling dope for the past several months, supplying friends and associates of yours and of your crew members, Carole and Dwayne?"

"Wha—?"

"Meaghan, the man who has been following you followed you for longer than you thought. You said you noticed him about two months ago. He had been following you for three months. He was assigned by the Federal Narcotics Bureau because they'd been keeping an eye on Carole and Dwayne, but it appeared you had become the major bag person."

Her jaw hung. "Philip, I don't even know what a bag person is!"

"It's the delivery person, the one who makes most of the drops, collects the money, all that."

"That's not true! I've never done that. I would *never* do that!"

"Meaghan, that woman who seemed to know Perkins tonight, had you ever seen her before?"

"No. She is Carole's aunt, and, and—" It had started to sink in. Now she spoke softly, in a monotone. "Philip, I've run a lot of errands for Carole. In fact, I've run a couple for Dwayne. You're not telling me—"

I nodded.

"Oh no," she said, whimpering. 'Oh no, no, no—"

I tried to remember to watch my speed in my haste to find a phone. Every time I saw a squad car I stiffened. Tiny Meaghan was now almost completely doubled over, her face resting between her knees, her hands on the back of her head as if she was accomplishing some off-the-wall gymnastics move. I had so many questions, but I assumed she did too, especially if she was for real. And I believed she was. Either that, or as Wally would have said, "I been taken."

Several minutes later, at a gas station on Touhy, I called the office. Wally answered before it had rung once. "Philip?" he said.

"Yeah, Wal—"

"Just tell me if she's with you and where you are."

"Yes. And Touhy, west of Ridge."

"Go directly to the Holiday Inn in Evanston. You know the place?"

"Yeah."

"Park in the underground garage and come to the elevator. Margo will bring you up to our rooms." And he hung up.

I could only guess they'd heard it all on the evening news and were waiting for my call. When we pulled into the dark garage at the Holiday Inn, less than an hour had passed since I heard the muffled crack of the shots and saw Jules Perkins hit the floor.

Margo was waiting near a railing outside the elevators. She held the door for us. Meaghan carried under her arm the cap and jacket she would likely never wear again. Margo said nothing; she just embraced me tightly and looked warily at Meaghan, then at the floor. I realized that she, and probably Wally too, still assumed Meaghan was guilty of murder.

Margo used her key to open the hotel room door on the sixth floor, and as we entered, Wally stood quickly and opened one of the doors that led to the adjoining room. He handed me the key and told me to run out and around to the other room and do the same from the other side. He looked glum.

I opened the adjoining door from the other side just as Wally was sizing up Meaghan. He roughly took her cap and jacket and dug around in the pockets. "Search her," he said to Margo.

"Oh, Wally," I said, "I don't think that's necess—"

"Yeah? You don't, huh, Spence? Did *you* search her?"

"No, but—"

"No, but nothin'! You think I got this far in a bad business by bein' stupid? You're lucky you're still standin' there, boy. This girl'd like to blow your head off as look at you."

"Wally—" I said.

"Mr. Festschrift," Meaghan whined.

"Lemme ask you somethin', Spence," Wally plunged on "You see this woman kill a man tonight?"

"No, I—"

"Can you swear she didn't?"

"Well, no. Perkins was blocking my view when—"

"Philip—" Meaghan began.

Wally ignored her. "Perkins was blockin' your view? Then you saw him hit the deck!" I nodded. "You like that, Spence? That exciting for you, boy? That man was a professional, and we go back a long way. He's careful. He does things right. But he got wasted tonight, didn't he? And we don't know whether this little thing did it or not. But you bring her back, forty-five minutes from the airport, and you don't know if she's got another weapon on her or not!"

"She's clean," Margo said quietly.

"Sit down," Wally told Meaghan, as if talking to a dog. He breathed a heavy sigh, collecting himself. "You were lucky, Philip," he said, more calmly now. "Stupid, but lucky." And I knew he was right.

Though the doors between the rooms were both open, we sat in the first room and left the second dark. "Now then," Wally began, as if class were in session, "start from when you hung up from talking to Margo. Did you ever decide whether Perkins had flown back from Boston with you?"

"You knew this guy," Meaghan said, announcing it as the revelation it was to her.

"I'll get to you, OK?" Wally said.

"I'm your client," she said, whining again.

"You're a fugitive we're harboring, if you want to know the truth of it," he said. "Whether you're guilty of murdering a federal agent or you're clean as a whistle, we're already in big trouble with you."

Meaghan hid her eyes with her hand.

"To answer your question, Wally, yes, I decided that Perkins had *not* flown back with us. I'm guessing he jumped onto the next flight back to Chicago from Boston. We weren't on the ground long there, so he had to have hurried and been lucky or flown on a private plane. I didn't see him get off, and I *did* see him come out of that little bar to follow Meaghan at O'Hare."

"OK, so then you followed him?" I nodded. "Did he know it?"

And I told Wally everything.

"I don't think Perkins told anyone that you were on that plane, Philip," Wally said.

"How do you know?"

"I don't know. I said I don't think he did. I know Perkins. He said he wouldn't if we agreed not to send anyone, and I gotta think he didn't tell anyone when we agreed *to* send someone just to make sure Meaghan went."

Meaghan gasped. "This was all set up by *you?* You *knew* what was going on and didn't tell me? I can't believe this!"

"Yeah, and you're about to sit there and tell us *you* didn't know what was going on, aren't you?"

"Yes, but—"

"Yes, but you *really* didn't know, right? Don't you think we might find *that* hard to believe? Now, Philip, we've got to settle this before I call the feds—"

"You're going to call them?" Meaghan said, amazed. "I wanted to go back and straighten it out when we first heard it on the radio, but Philip wouldn't. If it wasn't right to talk to them then, why is it OK now? And if *you* don't believe me, why should they?"

"Trust me, girl, *they* won't. And if we aren't convinced by the time I think we've harbored you too long—which was about five minutes ago—you're not gonna have *any* friends when they get here."

"They're coming here? Oh, please!"

"Something you wanna tell us? Something you wanna confess?"

"No! Of course not! I just want to be sure you're with me and believe me before you'd let anyone come and take me."

"Why do you think we've got two rooms here? We're gonna give you the benefit of the doubt, but so far all I've got is that we know you've sold dope several times over the past few weeks, sometimes to undercover agents and other times while witnessed by them.

"Tonight you're in the middle of it when a big buy goes down and somebody gets blown away, and a lot of eyewitnesses say you did it. But I'm lucky. I've got one of my people on the scene, so he can set me straight, only *he* doesn't know. The dead man got in his line of vision. He saw you, he saw Perkins's back, he hears chink-chink, he sees your bag and a gun slide by, and what have I got? Nothin' too pretty, I can tell ya that. Tell me, Miss Hanekamp, what would *you* believe?"

She shook her head and cried again.

"That's a nice bit," Wally said coldly. "But it's getting us, and particularly you, nowhere. Agh! I don't even want to know what kind of gyrations they're goin' through to try to find you. I gotta call somebody."

"But what do you think? I have to know you believe me! I knew nothing about this. I never even suspected; you have to believe me."

"Philip?"

"I believe her, Wally. If she was faking it in the car, well, then she's—"

"I know. She's the best in the business. Well, I for one don't wanna be the victim of the best in the business. Margo?"

"I don't know yet, Wally."

I couldn't resist an angry doubletake.

"I'm sorry, Philip. I know you have excellent judgment, but I wasn't in the car when the report came over the radio. And she could have been building up to that response. She had to know you were going to turn the radio on and that it would come out."

"But I didn't! From what you're all saying here, you knew long before *I* did. Why didn't you tell me and protect me from this? That's what I was paying you to do."

"Think of it from our side, Meaghan," Margo tried.

"That's not as easy as it sounds, Margo," she said. "You're not suspected of murdering someone. Have you ever seen somebody get shot right in front of you?"

Margo shook her head. "But Meaghan, when we checked you out a little and found you were under suspicion for selling drugs, we *had* to stay out of the way of the federal authorities. We tried to get out of even being on that plane, but then you wouldn't have gone and that would have spoiled their stake-out."

"Then that woman was working for *them?*"

"Of course."

"Then was *Carole* working for them? She's the one who told me where to find the woman and what she would be wearing and what to say to her."

"Why did she tell you all that?"

"That's how we always run each other's errands. Carole said she had a message for her aunt and her aunt had something for her, but she couldn't get off the plane."

"And that didn't make you suspicious?"

"No. Carole is our crew chief, and she's often too busy to get off during short layovers."

"What were you supposed to say to the woman?"

"I was just supposed to say, 'Are you?' and she would say, 'Yes.' And then I would say, 'This is from Carole,' and she would say, 'And this is *for* Carole.' And that was that."

"There was never any conversation, like you'd expect when you meet someone's relative, like their asking how she is or you're asking how they are related or anything?"

"Sometimes. But there was never much time. It was always between flights. If there was more time, Carole ran her own errands."

"Uh-huh," Wally said. "I'll just bet she did. Did Carole or Dwayne ever run any errands for you?"

"Of course."

"Like what?"

"Carole dropped something off for me in Michigan once. And there were other times."

"Did you know that that transaction was witnessed by federal authorities, and that they had to apologize to your mother for searching the package? They were embarrassed when it was only some souvenirs from L.A."

"She never told me that."

"She was warned not to. I'm sure it's been very difficult for her."

"Even my mother got into this?" She was crying again.

Wally peppered her with questions, tough questions, for another hour or so, never letting up, making her suffer, trying to push her to the point where she would realize the trouble she was in and giving her a few ways out if she wanted to give herself up and admit she had been in the middle of it by her own knowledge since the beginning.

When she didn't break, Wally looked up at Margo. She cocked her head and nodded. "I believe her," Margo said.

"So do I," Wally said. "You're gonna win the gullible girl of the year award. And I've still got to make the call."

Chapter Ten

Cedric Maxwell, head of the Chicago regional office of the Federal Narcotics Bureau, was a short, trim, graying man, impeccably dressed. And intense.

He had recognized Wally Festschrift's last name from Wally's years on the Chicago police force, so he wasn't about to pass off Wally's news as a crank call. Mr. Maxwell arrived in less than forty minutes. He was alone.

Margo and Meaghan were in the adjoining room with the double doors closed between us. The amenities were brief, and Maxwell took the floor, but not for long. He was smooth and seemed to enjoy using inflated language, which he constantly defined as he went along.

"I'm not going to attempt to intimidate, ah, bully, you sergeant," he began. "And I can only surmise that you have some sort of justification, a, uh, reason if you will, to harbor a woman who could presently turn up on the FBI's ten most-wanted list."

"I do. That's because we believe she's innocent."

"If she's innocent, Sergeant Festschrift, she has nothing to fear. I very much appreciate your informing me that you know of her whereabouts, but I really must insist that you let me know the specifics now. I have, on the strength of your very fine reputation, called off the area-wide bulletin, which has saved us a great deal of human and financial resources, time, and money. I could have wished you had seen your way clear to contact us earlier, but again, I presume you feel you had cause."

"Uh, yeah, Max—they call you Max, don't they?"

"Few do."

"Good, ah, Max, if our client has so little to fear, how come she could wind up on the most-wanted list?"

"Surely we don't have to start from the beginning, do we, Sergeant? You are well aware of what transpired at the airport tonight. You are, I must confess, the first individual I have heard from who believes the young woman did *not* fire upon our man. The only fingerprints available on her were from a checking account thumbprint verification, but that print clearly matches a print taken from the barrel of the weapon. Perhaps you'd like to tell me why you maintain her innocence."

"First of all, she told us someone else shot Perkins and then tossed her the gun. That would make sense based on what you just said. Right- or left-handed, her right thumbprint would not show up on the *barrel* of a gun she was shooting, would it?"

"That's for the jurists to decide, the courts. All we know is that the clearest print on the murder weapon belongs to Meaghan Hanekamp, and many witnesses place her at the scene of the crime."

"Including one of our own."

"Pardon me?"

"This man here was at the scene."

"Mr. Spence? What were you doing there?"

"Keeping our client under surveillance, as we were paid to do."

"Were you aware that she was under surveillance by our office?"

I looked to Wally.

"We prefer not to answer that at this time."

Maxwell was becoming edgy. "Mr. Festschrift, you are not in a position to be telling me what you will or will not answer."

"I'm not, huh? OK then, we *don't* know where your suspect is."

Maxwell glared at Wally.

"You wanna tell me who's in what position to do what, Max? Seems to me, we're in the driver's seat here. You can bring me up on charges and I can forget I ever called you in the first place. Then what've you got? You've got me inconvenienced by havin' to go downtown a while while you guys try to prove I'm hidin' somebody you want. Meanwhile, your suspect could be out of the country. You think stewardesses don't have access to free rides? She wouldn't even have to take it in her own name."

"She'd better not."

"She wouldn't need to. They trade 'em, sell 'em, you name it."

"We're getting nowhere, Sergeant. If you're not going to cooperate, why did you call me?"

"We wanna cooperate. We just want to make sure Meaghan gets a fair shake. From everything you've said, it sounds like you've got her locked up, open and shut."

"I'd be deceiving you if I tried to tell you otherwise."

"Awright then, all I want from you is an open mind. I wanna tell you a story, and it's gonna sound a little, um, lu—?"

"Ludicrous?"

"Right! I knew you'd know the word I was after. It's gonna sound ludicrous at first, but I want you to at least start with an open mind. OK?"

"It's the least I can do."

"Awright, we're talkin' here about a straight young woman. She's a stewardess, or whatever it is they call themselves nowadays. An'—"

"Flight attendants," Cedric Maxwell submitted.

"Whatever. Anyway, she's the first girl from her hometown to make it as one of these attendees things, and she's tryin' to make Mom and Dad proud. She's got a bum of a little brother who's up to no good, but even she doesn't know how bad that egg is. She thinks he's just a no-account who's moochin' off Mom and Dad, but he's actually a head, into dope and all the creeps that go with it. I'm bettin' Mom and Dad know and aren't tellin' her, OK?"

I could have sworn Maxwell rolled his eyes, but Wally took it as encouragement.

"So in her first few years on the job, our girl doesn't get *more* worldly-wise; she gets *less*. When she runs into lowlifes, even high-level lowlifes now, like she's not used to—you understand, in her life, the bad guys look like it, dress like it, act like it, or are little brothers and don't know any better—she pulls a little farther back into her shell. When the bad guys turn out to be men from the cockpit or the cabin, she doesn't catch on. She thinks they're just creeps who slipped by everyone else, so she rats on 'em.

"On the first crew she's with, she gets a navigator in trouble. The guy's been comin' on to the ladies for years, and most of 'em just shut him down. If they happen to be a shade loose, he's in luck. But if they're straight or tough, he gives up. With our little lady, he's intrigued by her naive act, only it's not an act. You with me so far, Max?"

Maxwell nodded disgustedly and looked at his watch.

"Secretly, all the other ladies are glad to see the navigator get his comeuppance, but now they won't have a thing to do with small-town-girl. She can't understand that. A gay co-worker tells her he's sorry he ever admitted anything to her and begs her not to say anything. She tells him she *will* if he ever tries anything with a passenger or crew member, and he tells her what he thinks of that. She's just bein' honest, and she's gettin' kicked in the shins.

"You think she's growin' from this, learning a few things? Wouldn't you guess she'd catch on, wise up, mature, develop a little uptown sense? Nah! This small-town streak runs deep. She gets on another crew and she falls in love with someone, and he's not in love with her. Happens to everybody, right? Well, it hadn't happened to her before.

"She'd believed all her life that Mr. Right would come boppin' along some day, and when he bops along, she wants to hang on. It doesn't work out, so what does she do? She *wants* to head back home, but will she? No. Little brother does *that* type of stuff. She's not gonna be a failure. She's not gonna run home to Mommy. It was the stewardessing or the, uh, the whatever, that got her where she was. She'd stick it out. She'll get transferred yet again maybe, but she won't quit.

"Problem was, 'course, that there is no small town

in the flight game. And there aren't too many choices for girls who ask for lots of transfers. They quit lettin' *you* choose where you're gonna go. So they tell her, 'All right, you want a new crew, a new city to fly out of, here's where we need ya,' only it's Chicago.

"She's not sure what she thinks about that, but it *is* closer to home than anywhere else she'd been based, so she takes it. She has to get away from that second crew, or that guy anyway, so she comes to the big city. She finds the best, most secure, most convenient apartment she can, not even realizing that she coulda done just as well if not better an' stayed closer to the airport. But Chicago is Chicago, so she gets a place with a doorman and lots of security and a parking garage and all that, and she moves in. Only this girl is so naive, she misses the point that the space for her car costs another bunch a month until she's already signed the lease and moved in.

"Now the place costs her so much she's hardly got anything to live on, but she doesn't care. All she cares about is trying to get next to the new crew. Bein' a sports nut and a former high school track star, she thinks she's died and gone to heaven when she finds out how many baseball games are on TV in Chicago. You know why she's so glad they're on TV? Because she hasn't met anybody yet who'll go with her to the ballparks, and she doesn't feel like she should go alone. She might get lost or mugged or whatever, and who wants to go alone, anyway?

"I know what you're thinkin', Max"—but from the look on Maxwell's face, I was sure Wally didn't —"you're thinkin' I gotta be crazy to think a woman can be a big-time stewardess and not feel confident about findin' her way around big cities. But think about it. If she can get herself to the airport and to the gate every day, and if she can follow the other people to the right hotels and maybe hang around with 'em a little in the other cities, she doesn't have to be a woman of the world. She doesn't have to know anything but what makes passengers feel safe and happy. In fact, some of that fresh naivete is charming to the people.

"This girl charmed my socks off when I first met her, Max, and if you think she did a number on me, well, don't think I didn't think the same. I gave it to her good and tough, the way you would have if I know you, and I think I do. I pushed her, I pressured her, I doubted her. And when she told me she'd been followed around by a guy for several weeks, it sounded bad to me.

"I mean, it sounded fishy, you know? 'Course you know, you've heard all the stories before. Woman knows why she's bein' hassled but she runs for help and pretends not to know why, so you protect her, maybe rough somebody up, and you find out in the end she deserved it all along. I didn't want that to happen, first case after I take over for Earl Haymeyer. You know Earl, huh?"

"Of course."

"Yeah, sure, of course. So anyway, I gotta be honest with ya. When she described the guy, I knew it was Perkins. I was at the range that day back in the sixties when he messed up his finger in that firing pin, you remember that? No? You weren't in Chicago then? 'Course not, FNB didn't have a Chicago office then, did they?

"Anyway, I figure it's Perkins. I don't just figure, I know, OK? And so I tell my people, I says, 'This gal here is one of the best in the business or they don't put Perkins on her trail,' right? I tell 'em she's a con artist and she's gonna get busted and all the rest, and so we better back off.

"I gotta hand it to my people though, Max. They believed her. They bought the package. They had spent time with her. They thought she was for real. They knew it was a long shot because she was some creation, but they weren't convinced until, well, now I guess I gotta tell ya, and I don't s'pose it can get Julie in any trouble now, but, ah, I gave him a call. I had him come in. I told him all about it.

"I know what you're thinkin' Max, but you woulda been proud of him, really you would. In fact, ha ha, he acted a little like you're actin' right now. I mean, he didn't want to give us a thing. He figured Meaghan Hanekamp was none of our concern, and he wanted me to tell whatever local agency had put us up to trailin' her that you guys had it all under control. He wasn't any cooler when he heard that no one had put us up to it but us. She was our client, but he guessed that if we knew enough, we'd back off the case.

"It was a logical assumption, Max, but it couldn't work. Oh, I guess in one way it worked. Those stories of his, about sweet innocent Meaghan delivering dope and takin' big bucks, well, we all believed 'em. We all, I think to a man, well, to two of us it was to a man and to one of us it was to a woman—to a person, we got ourselves convinced that we'd been had.

"I'd been had before, haven't you? Yeah, me too.

And I didn't want it to happen again, especially by someone who was shovelin' such a huge load of baloney. One of the reasons my people believed her from the beginning—and I gotta tell ya, much as I hate to admit it, I didn't—was because she was so simple and naive that it had to be true. But I'll tell ya another thing that has always stuck in my craw. Why did she seek us out so, ah, so aggressively?

"I mean, if she was just tryin' to protect herself from you and look good as a secret little drug pusher, she coulda just hired her own eyewitnesses to testify for her, or got some local muscle to work on Perkins. But she was sincere; she had to be. She looked my people up when she really got scared, and if she was guilty of what you people think she was, she had to know it would all come out and make her look worse than ever.

"And you know how she looked 'em up? She tracked 'em a coupla days through real estate agencies and interrupted their honeymoon, forevermore. If you're just hirin' somebody to cover your own tracks, do you do something like that, something that could put you on their bad side for the rest of your life?"

Cedric Maxwell had taken about all he could take. "Sergeant Festschrift," he said wearily, "you are a most interesting and even entertaining filibusterer. Perhaps not as convincing as you might hope, but entertaining nonetheless. If you're trying to starve me out, you're doing a good job. You might bore me to death too. Are you getting to any point, or is there no end to this?"

"Are you hungry, Max, because if you are, it'd be my privilege, it really would. I don't have far to go here in my little story, but just say the word if you could use a burger or anything at all—"

"No, Sergeant. The very news that you haven't far to go has so fortified me that I believe I'll survive this."

"Does that mean you *do* want a sandwich, or that you don't?"

"I don't, thank you. Very much."

"Awright, suit yerself. So this girl finds my people, tells 'em a scary story, shows 'em more gullibility than they've seen since they met each other—get it?—and they drag her back to me to see what we're gonna do with her. So, as I told you, I don't buy it. I hear what I think means Perkins is involved. I bring him in, get him riled, even let him listen in to her on the phone.

"First, and you'll be glad to hear this, he tries to scare me off by tellin' me he'll bring me up on charges if we follow through on our promise to the girl to protect her from you-know-who on her next flight. Then he hears that she won't go unless we send somebody, so he gives in, says one of us can go.

"But you know what really got to all of us, all of us except Jules, I mean? She says she's seen her tail recently out her apartment window, and all the time he's been with us. If he hadn't changed our minds with all his stories of her pickups and deliveries, she's iced it with what sounded like a lie.

"But I can tell by the look on your face, Max, that you did have somebody at her place today, didn't you?"

"Do I have to answer that?"

"I told *you* something I wasn't gonna tell ya. Anyway, you just answered it. You had somebody there. In fact, I'm guessin' that except on the plane rides, Meaghan Hanekamp might have seen two or three guys she thought were one and the same. Am I right? Of course I'm right.

"So she wasn't lyin' about that. My man goes, to help Perkins out some, and he's really intending not to follow her. But Jules crosses him up, stays off the plane in Boston. Meaghan, the suspicious interstate drug trafficker, is so fooled by this big move that she decides he's not going to show up again until, say, L.A. So, without a second thought, and after makin' clear to my guy that she doesn't need to be followed or protected, she waltzes right through O'Hare to a big, not so carefully planned setup. It doesn't wash, Max."

"Festschrift, you can't avoid the fact that people say she shot Perkins."

"What people? My guy was closer to her than anyone except Jules, and he says he didn't see her with the gun. He also says he saw someone running out one of the gate doors behind the scene. The girl saw him too. She screamed his name when he tossed her the gun. His name was Dwayne."

And for the first time, Maxwell flinched. "Dwayne?" he repeated.

"Dwayne. He works with her on the crew. Oh, don't give me that, Max. If you guys have been on her trail for months, you know who Dwayne is."

"Of course we do. What about him?"

"What about him? He snuffed Perkins, that's what about him. Your backup men—Philip only saw two, so you musta thought this gig was gonna go down without too much trouble—didn't see Dwayne, so they couldn't have seen the murder. You ask 'em if they saw Meaghan with a gun pointed at Jules. If they didn't, all you've got is people who heard shots, saw a man fall, and saw Meaghan running for her life. Of course, we both know who can really clear Meaghan. Tell me about your woman on the scene, Max."

"She'll do you no good, Sergeant. It was only her third job. She was nervous, and she doesn't know what happened. When Perkins signaled her to drop to the floor, she collapsed and saw nothing. She admits that when she last saw Meaghan, she had no weapon. But Meaghan *had* been putting the envelope she'd just received back into her bag. She could have come back up with the gun."

"It's a long shot, Max, and you know it."

"Maybe, but not as long as some of the stuff you've been trying to pass off on me. On what are you really basing your defense of this woman?"

"It might sound a bit weak, and I told you from the beginning that it would also sound ludicrous in spots—"

"And it has."

"You haven't exactly won any awards tonight yerself, Max."

"When have I had the chance?"

"Awright, let me answer your question. I trust my people, and I trust my own judgment, though I almost blew it on this one. They believe her. Spence bases it on her reaction to the news when she finally heard on the radio what had happened out there tonight. Margo, that's my investigator gal, she believes her because—plain and simple—Meaghan convinced her."

"And you, Sergeant? What changed your mind? You were skeptical of her from the beginning."

"I thought you'd never ask. I believe her because of somethin' so basic, it might make you laugh. I believe her because I believe *in* her. If I'm gettin' taken this time, it really *is* by the best in the business. This girl is for real, Max. And you know something? I been in this game a long time, longer'n you, prob'ly. And there's something consistent about her story, right from the beginning. She's never had to backtrack, cover herself, change her story, or explain anything. To her it's all made perfect sense, because she was telling the truth as she knew it.

"She didn't know until after the man was dead that Jules Perkins was a federal drug agent, or that he suspected her of being a pusher. That's it right on the table, Max."

"Well," Maxwell said slowly, rising. "I can't say I'm not impressed. I've followed your career for many years—your dogged pursuit of murderers and your interest in justice, even at the expense of your own advancement. You're a little rough around the edges, and I wouldn't have thought you could get far with this disorganized and embellished yarn of yours, but I have to say I appreciate your trying. And if I can tell you one thing more, a lot of people are behind you in your fight with the Chicago PD, because they know that whatever you did, against department policy or not, you had to have done it with justice in mind, and that's all that counts. So, I don't know what reason you have for defending Meaghan Hanekamp, other than a pure belief of her innocence. I'm afraid I can't act on your word, and that I'll have to insist now that you release her to me. But I do appreciate your speaking on her behalf. If there's any truth to it, I guarantee it will come out."

"For my trouble, you can at least tell me what was supposed to be going down tonight. I'm real curious about you only havin' three guys on a job like this one."

"We didn't know it was going to wind up like this, Wally."

"Better'n that, you thought it was gonna be a cake walk for some reason, and I wanna know the reason."

"You think you know the reason?"

"Yeah, I think I do."

"You want to take a stab at it?"

"Sure. I think the reason had a name. I think his name was Dwayne."

And Cedric Maxwell flinched again. Wally had him.

Chapter Eleven

Wally pretended not to notice that Mr. Maxwell had waxed uncomfortable. He turned away from the man for the first time since he had entered the room and asked politely if I would mind "callin' Miss Hanekamp from the phone down in the lobby and asking her if she remembers why her fellow crew member, Dwayne, was not on the flight back to Chicago from Boston on Saturday?"

But before I got out the door, wondering whether Maxwell would hear the phone ring in the next room in a few minutes, Wally said, "Ya see, Max, I have a crazy memory for details like these. One little thing I remembered from her story, and from Philip and Margo's account of their trip, was that Dwayne was not on that flight."

"Hold up a minute, Mr. Spence," Maxwell said. And Wally waved me back in.

But Wally wanted to push his point further before the federal man conceded anything. "He wasn't on the flight *to* Boston this afternoon, either, was he, Phil?"

I started to shake my head, but Maxwell answered for me. "No, he wasn't." He appeared ready to give Wally more, but Wally wanted to keep pressing so Maxwell wouldn't stop with a morsel. He wanted the whole story.

"And I imagine, though I'm only guessin' here, that he wasn't on the flight *back* from Boston, either, was he?" And Maxwell shook his head again. "Still speculatin' now, but could Dwayne have been in Boston for some reason, waitin' for Perk—"

"No, no, you've got that wrong now, Festschrift."

"He wasn't waitin' in Boston for Perkins and then the two of them fly back together for a set up?"

"No, that would have been too costly and unnecessary, and too risky."

"Ah, it was too risky! You didn't *need* Dwayne to be in Boston, because Perkins could call him from there to tell him how everything was going and to find out if there were any hitches on his end. And you didn't *want* Dwayne around because you didn't know how to bust both him *and* Carole when it was Carole and Meaghan you really wanted."

"All right, Wally. I'm going to tell you how it was, but I must have your guarantee that at the end of this, you return Meaghan Hanekamp to my custody. Is it a deal?"

Wally moved from a chair to the bed and stretched his bulk out as far as it would go. He kicked his shoes off and put his hands behind his head. He smiled, but only slightly. The weight of the death of an old friend still pressed upon him. "What you're about to tell me is going to all but exonerate my client, Max. I want to get it good and enjoy it."

"But you *will* give me Miss Hanekamp?"

"Of course. You won't be able to hurt her then."

"I wouldn't have hurt her anyway, Wally. You know that."

"I also know how the bureaucracy works, Max.

Once it gets a naive little thing like Meaghan in its jaws, it chews her up, makes mincemeat out of her by using her as a scapegoat for a bungled operation, protects all its people and its informants and its rats—like Dwayne—and then it spits her out, who knows where? A federal penitentiary somewhere."

"Wally," Cedric Maxwell said, pained, "you can't really think I'd stand by and let that happen to an innocent person."

"You're admitting she's innocent? You say that and you can have her for questioning right now."

"I was merely reacting to your hypothetical situation. I cannot commit myself on the guilt or innocence of Miss Hanekamp."

"Awright, OK, just tell me how it was. What really went down?"

Maxwell called his car from a radio in his pocket, telling his associates that he wouldn't be long and that they should arrange for a local police matron to accompany them back to the city with a female subject.

"We've been working on this case for nearly a year. Our favorite and least favorite target is this Dwayne Lindgren, because while he's been a terrific informant, he's the lowest of the low. It's our own fault. We offered him immunity if he'd turn on his people, but the catch was, he had to give us everybody.

"He'd been doing pretty well, letting us know when things were happening, where, who, the whole thing. Problem was, he was giving us lots of good stuff on everybody but his girl friend."

"His girl friend?"

"Carole. They live together."

"I didn't know that. Why didn't Meaghan tell us that, Philip?"

"It could only be because she doesn't know. She hasn't kept anything else from us."

"You hope," Maxwell said. "Anyway, we tell him he's got to give us something on everybody, and that includes his lady. After a while we tell him we don't think he's got it in him to turn on her and that we'd better just call off the deal and bust him on what we had so far."

"What'd you have, Max?"

"A string of things. Both of them could have served time. Carole had never known she'd bought and sold from and to our people. But we got Dwayne once in Miami because he was dealing internationally."

"How do you mean you got him? You had to take him rather than just watch?"

"Correct."

Wally squinted at Maxwell. "Why?"

"As I told you, it was international. We were making an arrest of an illegal alien at the same time."

Wally still appeared skeptical. "You coulda done that without bustin' this Dwayne if he was still servin' your purpose. He knows you were onto him before that?"

"No, we don't think so."

"I don't think so, either. Why'd you really bust him, Max?"

"Let me get on with my story, Wally."

"Let *me* get on with my suspicions."

"Don't be too sure I can reveal everything you want, Wally. I'm already going farther than I should in this."

"As we've said, you don't have a choice."

"Oh, but I do. You want me to exercise it?"

"You want me to run with my suspicions and embarrass you in front of this young and impressionable detective, Max?"

"You save yours, and I'll save mine, OK?"

Wally smiled contentedly, knowing he had one more angle on Maxwell and Dwayne. Trouble was, he had one on me, too, because I didn't know what in the world he was driving at.

"Anyway, we felt we had to arrest Mr. Lindgren, but we gave him several options whereby he could improve his own situation. We were making good progress until we tripped over his reluctance to give us anything on Carole. We even offered to let him tell her what was going on and to encourage her to join with us as well, but he wanted a deal. He told us that if we could forget the buys and sells we had her on, he'd give us somebody bigger."

"Uh-huh."

"We were skeptical, but intrigued. We told him it would have to be pretty hot stuff for us to even consider such action, and that he would also have to guarantee us that both he and Carole were out of the racket for good."

"A bit of wishful thinking, eh, Max?"

"Well, Wally, you've been through this a time or two. You know you always take deals like that because these people are going to fall back into the game sooner or later, and then you can go after them hot and heavy because they're violating the sacred trust you put in them."

Both men smiled, and Maxwell continued. "There is always the exception who really does go straight, and then you have a double benefit. You've cleaned up part of the mess, and you've used him to help you get someone else."

"The way I see it," Wally said, "if you can use a guy to get somebody else, and then he screws up and you can get him too, *that's* the *real* benefit."

"But Wally, we all have to hold out hope that someone will change."

"That's the spirit. You sound like a youngster in the job. You ever see a creep like this Dwayne change?"

"Can't say that I have."

"So continue."

"He assures us they'll both be clean, that neither are users to start with—they were only in it for the money, which we feel is true to a point—and they're going to deliver a big connection to us on a silver platter."

"Meaghan Hanekamp."

"You got it."

"She was supposed to be getting her stuff from somewhere other than Carole and Dwayne?"

"That's what he wanted us to believe."

"But she always delivered the stuff to people who were supposed to be friends and acquaintances and relatives of Carole."

"That's what Dwayne wanted us to believe was the reason he would so gladly rat on her. He said she was using Carole's name in all the transactions and that that would make it tougher for us to believe Carole was now out of the business."

"And did it?"

"Sure. Her name popped up everywhere, but we felt that most of the time it *was* due to Meaghan Hanekamp's broadcasting it all over. Meaghan never made a deal in her own name. Most of the time she used Carole's for the pitch. Once she even used Dwayne's. Was he mad."

"How mad, Max?"

"Mad enough. Dwayne tipped us off on every deal Meaghan made, and we were there, either watching or involved."

"Tell me. Wasn't somethin' big comin' down here tonight with Dwayne out of the picture, maybe out of town? Were you just protecting your boy?"

"That was part of it. You've probably guessed the rest."

"My guess is you told Dwayne one thing and planned another. You told Dwayne you were gonna get Meaghan in a big one if he could tell you when and where it was happening. You'd had your people involved long enough that no matter who made the buy, it would cover you against Dwayne. Then you'd use Meaghan to get to Carole. Am I right?"

"Exactly. We were going to give Meaghan one chance to implicate Carole, without Dwayne's knowledge."

"So, how did he find out you were crossing him?"

"Who says he found out?"

"My eyewitness, and Meaghan."

"If Meaghan is so lily white, what does she know about any dealings we may have had with Dwayne?

And your man admits he just thought he saw somebody."

"Yeah, but Meaghan saw Dwayne. Meaghan screamed, "Dwayne." Meaghan wound up with Dwayne's gun in her hands, Max. You can't trace the gun, 'cause he's smart enough to use a hot one, but I was hittin' close to home on that international bust of yours, wasn't I?"

Maxwell didn't respond.

"Hm, Max?"

"I'm not going to hand it to you, Wally."

"But you'll tell me if I'm right?"

Again, Maxwell was silent.

"Max, you hadda bust Dwayne on the Miami gig 'cause he was carryin' a piece, right? And no matter what, you can't let a guy get on a plane, especially a bad guy like Lindgren and especially that close to Cuba and lotsa other international type places, when he's armed."

Cedric Maxwell swore. "Anybody ever tell you you oughta be a cop, Festschrift? You wouldn't even make a bad lawyer. C'mon, give me the girl."

"You gotta be kiddin'. I shouldn't give you a thing. Give it to me straight, pal. We're all in this thing together and all that, after the same thing, right? You want justice; I want justice. You want Dwayne, and all of creation knows I want him. I want him for Meaghan."

"This whole thing isn't as crystal clear in my mind as it is in yours, Wally."

"Whadya mean? You tellin' me it's not clear to a cop like you that Dwayne and Carole used Meaghan, takin' candy from her like the baby she is? You sayin' you can't tell that these two took you and your boys for a little joyride? Face it, Max. You blew it. Your people didn't expect to see Dwayne tonight, but Dwayne planned to be there all along to protect his honey.

"You were gonna nail Meaghan good, and it was gonna be so easy that you told Dwayne that the same guy who'd been on the plane all that time would be the only one involved. That was a mistake, because it made Dwayne think that snuffin' him and blaming it on Meaghan would be easier. He'd get back at you because he somehow learned or figured or guessed that you weren't really protecting his woman and that you must be after him eventually, too. And he could make you think he was straight about Meaghan bein' such a baddie if he could make her look like more than a peddler, but a murderer too."

Now Maxwell was angry, but he didn't even try to refute Wally's thesis. "What do you want, Wally? You want me to fall to my knees and say I'm to blame for Perkins's death? Do you? Because that's how I feel. You think I need someone like you, who probably could have handled it better or at least wouldn't have trusted a pusher as far as we trusted Lindgren, to sit there and tell me I blew it? All right, I blew it. And I hate it. And it's going to work on me for a long, long time. So lay off me, OK, Wally?"

Wally hunched himself up to a sitting position and lurched off the bed to stand next to Maxwell. "OK, Max," he said gently. "OK, you're right. I took it too far. We all have things we gotta live with. I just don't wanna live with this innocent girl on my conscience, that's all. And don't blame yourself for

Perkins. You musta thought twice about it at the last minute, since a coupla other guys were there. Was that your idea?"

Maxwell nodded.

"There, see? You did all you could. I don't know what else you coulda done, not expecting Dwayne. You had 'em placed right too, because if Lindgren had seen 'em, it would have blown the whole thing."

"I'd rather have blown the whole thing and be set back for months in the investigation if it meant Perkins didn't have to take it tonight."

"I hear ya. But you know there's still something we can do for Perkins. We can get an innocent little girl out of a pile of trouble. And we can get Dwayne."

"Wally, I like your story, and I'd like to buy the whole package, but all I've got are your speculations about something we saw totally differently during one of the most intensive surveillance operations I've ever conducted."

"But you know Dwayne was packin' a heater as far back as Miami. That and the fact that Meaghan saw him tonight ices him, doesn't it?"

"Only if Meaghan is totally clean, and all I have is your optimism on that."

"C'mon, Max, I gave you more than that."

"Maybe, and I don't like what it looks like, but—"

"Do this for me, at least, Max. As fast as you can, get in touch with all your people. Ask them to consider the possibility, to just think about the chance that this Meaghan Hanekamp they bought from or sold to, was one hundred percent set up. Ask 'em if they ever once had a conversation with her that would rule out that chance. If she ever talked deals or price or quality of dope or danger or anything like that with even one of 'em, then my theory's down the drain, out the window, gone."

Maxwell didn't respond, but he didn't appear closed to the idea either. Wally kept the pressure on. "It can't hurt, Max. And it wouldn't be that difficult to poll 'em, would it?"

"Probably not."

"Do it, Max. Do it for me. Nuts, do it for Perkins. And do it for Meaghan. We owe her that much. Can you imagine what we owe her, all of us, I mean, all the brothers under the badge, if she's clean?"

"Do you know what a rare bird, an incredibly naive person, she would have to be to be totally clean, Wally?"

Wally smiled. "Yeah. She'd be a first all right. But she's solid."

Maxwell folded his arms and gazed around the room. He sighed. Wally watched him intently, then spoke as softly as I had ever heard him. 'Max. I don't wanna push you, pal. And I know I been a little hard on ya tonight. I also know you could have my skin with some of the stuff I've pulled, and you went out of your way to cater to me and all that. I 'preciate it, 'cause I think you thought I was good for it. You gave me the benefit of the doubt. Now, I don't wanna rush you or make like I'm in charge, 'cause all that stuff about not givin' you a choice and bein' in the driver's seat and everything, well I think you know that's just my way of gassin'. So let's forget all that. Now I'm askin' ya as a fellow professional, do this checkin' for me, for Perkins, for the girl, and do it quick. It's gettin' late, and the longer we let this scum Lindgren stay on the street, the more mess we might hafta clean up come daybreak. Who knows where him and his girlfriend might be by then? Let's get 'im, Max. That's all I'm askin'. If somethin' turns up that burns my story, then that'll be that. Whadya say?"

Chapter Twelve

Over the course of the past several weeks, seven undercover agents from the Federal Narcotics Bureau had had at least some direct contact with Meaghan Hanekamp. Cedric Maxwell called them from the phone in Wally Festschrift's hotel room and basically walked each through the same conversation:

"I'm sorry to bother you at home, but we're at a crucial juncture here in the Lindgren-Hanekamp-TransCoastal case. . . . Yes, you heard? . . . I understand Mrs. Perkins is taking it pretty hard, as you could imagine. . . . No, we haven't actually taken Hanekamp into custody, but that should come within a matter of an hour or so. Listen, I need some very important information from you, if you could bear with me just a moment. Feel free to refer to your notes or your copy of your report if necessary.

"What I need to know is this: If all we had to go on in prosecuting Hanekamp was what she said during any of the transactions or arrangements for transactions, would we have a case? Would we have anything on her? . . . I know what you heard on the news, and we'd all like to nail whoever did this to Perkins—no, I'm afraid it's not quite as simple as the news reports make it sound. Believe me, if there's a shred of evidence, we'll get her, but you must put tonight out of your mind for a moment if you can.

"I need to know very specifically from you if, based on your personal experience with Hanekamp, she incriminated herself by what she said. Limit it only to anything she might have actually said. . . . Sure, I can wait. In fact, let me call you back in a few minutes."

The dapper Mr. Maxwell had removed his suitcoat and loosened his tie, and now he sat in slacks and vest on the corner of a dressing table, the phone in his lap, his head bowed in concentration. He spoke with each contact with his eyes closed, going back over his list in the same order he had called them in the first place.

"It's me again," he began. "What can you tell me? . . . Yes, uh-huh, uh-huh. . . . This is from Carole, this is for Carole, yeah. Anything else? . . . OK, right. Uh-huh. . . . That's it, huh? . . . Well, I really don't know at this point, but that's a possibility. . . . No, I really can't get into it right now, but no one's going to get away with anything, you can rest assured of that. Anything else at all? . . . No? . . . No, I understand. . . . Well, maybe. We just might have, but keep this quiet until you hear from me."

Maxwell appeared to be almost in tears by the third such call. They each took pretty much the same pattern. Apparently the people who had been working to solidify the case against Meaghan were unable to implicate her with direct quotes, but each wanted to be sure she suffered for killing Perkins. None wanted to entertain the possibility that perhaps she was not what they all assumed she was.

By the last few calls, Wally was sitting on the edge of the bed, leaning forward with his elbows on his knees, listening intently. Maxwell held the phone to his ear with one hand and rested his forehead in the other, almost as if asleep. His voice seemed to betray more emotion as he continued his phone work.

During the last call, Wally stood and listened for any difference in Maxwell's response. When he was confident his point had been proved and that no surprises would disappoint him, he stepped to the double doors separating the rooms, knocked twice, and stepped a couple of feet into the other room when Margo answered his knock.

With a gesture, he silently beckoned Meaghan to join us. She entered cautiously, eyes puffy, face red. Her hair was mussed, and she had replaced her uniform jacket but had not buttoned it. Her trembling fingers showed the tension.

Margo followed and leaned back against the adjoining doors. She motioned me to her with her head. "You won't believe this," she whispered, "but we've been praying together."

"You're kidding!"

"Told you you wouldn't believe it."

"She's—?"

"No, but she's searching. Wouldn't you be, in a situation like this? She was raised in a churchy family, Philip. Not Christians, but she sure seems to know the score. I just asked her if she would mind if I prayed for her. She was eager."

Wally pointed to a chair not three feet from where Maxwell's feet dangled off the edge of the dressing table, and Meaghan carefully sat down. Hands folded, she looked tentatively at Maxwell. He was hardly aware of her, his head still bowed to his chest, eyes closed, finishing his last conversation.

He hung up slowly, leaving his hand on the receiver and staring at it. He let his hand slide off the phone and entwined his fingers between his knees, leaning forward as if to rest from the ordeal. With a quick sigh, he deliberately raised his head, his bloodshot eyes finally looking deep into Meaghan's.

"Young lady," he said hoarsely, "it appears we may owe you an enormous apology." Wally stood behind her and gently rested his hands on her heaving shoulders as she sobbed.

After a few minutes, Wally spoke quietly to Cedric Maxwell. "You got enough on this Carole to put her away when you find her?"

"Sure. We're betting she'll either try to hole up in L.A. at the end of this flight from Chicago, or she'll try to return on some other flight immediately, getting into Chicago in the wee hours."

"Let's not sweat her, then," Wally suggested. "Let's use Meaghan to get to Lindgren." They moved into the other room to map out strategy, returning in about twenty minutes with a plan that required Meaghan's help.

"I know it's more than we should ask after all you've been through," Maxwell said. "But if you'd like to get a dope peddler and a murderer off the streets, maybe some of this will have been worth it."

"I'll do what I can," she said weakly. "But I'm not in very good shape right now."

"Believe it or not, that's not all bad," Maxwell

said. "Dwayne isn't going to expect you to be in a party mood."

Wally outlined what she was to do while Maxwell radioed his men and requested certain paraphernalia that would not only tape a phone conversation, but would also amplify it to a speaker box. Within another half hour, Meaghan was ready, though still shaky.

"Don't try to hide your emotions," Maxwell advised.

"I don't think I could if I wanted to," she said.

The room was getting crowded with Maxwell and his two men, the equipment, Wally, Margo, Meaghan, and me. When everything was plugged in and the receiver lifted, we heard the dial tone. "I'm betting he's home and that he'll want us to believe he's been there all evening."

Meaghan hung up. "I'm not sure I can do this," she whined.

Maxwell looked frustrated, but Wally stood and held up a hand. "It's all right, Max. She'll do it. She just wants a minute to collect herself. This is the girl who was raised right. This is the girl who would rat on a gay friend if he tried anything funny with a co-worker or a passenger. This is the girl who got a navigator in trouble after he'd enjoyed years of gettin' away with a little too much of everything. She's gonna do it, Max. She's gonna have no trouble helpin' you put away a scoundrel like Dwayne. Jus' let her do it in her own time."

Meaghan pressed a tissue to her eyes and nose and forced a smile in spite of herself. "You know me, don't you?" she said.

"He knows *everybody*," Maxwell said. And everyone smiled. Meaghan was ready.

With the speaker phone back on and the tape rolling, all we heard after she dialed was a busy signal. Wally caught Maxwell's eyes. "Wonder what he's up to," he said. Maxwell shrugged.

"Let's give him a few minutes and try again," he said. "Unless he's left the phone off the hook, at least we know he's there."

"Or someone's there," Wally said. "Wouldn't have to be our man."

"Don't say that," Maxwell said. But after several more tries, Max took the phone and dialed the operator. "Yes, I've trying to dial a number for quite a while now and I'm getting a busy signal. Can you tell me if there's trouble on the line?" He gave her the number.

"One moment please, sir."

"Thank you."

After a moment: "There's conversation, sir."

"Thank you very much, operator."

"You're welcome, sir."

"You should have asked what they were saying," Margo said, and everyone laughed, breaking the tension again.

Ten minutes later, Meaghan dialed and got a ring. We all edged forward toward the speaker box. "Hello," came the surprisingly pleasant, next-door-neighbor-type voice of Dwayne Lindgren.

"Dwayne?"

"Yeah, who's this?"

"You know who this is."

"Meaghan? You sound upset."

"*You* don't."

"Should I be? What's happenin'?"

"You know what's happening, Dwayne. If you don't, you're the only one in Chicago who doesn't."

"All right, OK, I've been watching the news. What do you want from me?"

"Don't play games with me, Dwayne. I *saw* you shoot the man."

After a long pause: "Hey, I wasn't the one standin' there sellin' dope to a narc."

"Oh, you weren't? You don't think I know who I've been selling for? If it wasn't you, who was it?"

"Carole; who else?"

"Did she think I didn't know what was going on too?"

No reply.

"Did you both really think I would be naive enough to do all your dirty work and not expect anything in return?"

Still no reply. Meaghan waited him out.

"So what do you want, money?"

"I want to know what you thought you were trying to do tonight."

"I was just watchin' out for you. I blew the guy away, didn't I?"

"Sure, and now the whole town is looking for me. What am I supposed to do, Dwayne?"

"That's your problem."

"No, it isn't, Dwayne. I saw you. I know what you did. And if you don't help me stay hidden, or get me some money to get me out of here, as soon as they find me, I'll be telling them everything."

Silence.

"Dwayne, I left my bag at the airport. If I hadn't been able to snatch a purse on the way out, I never would have made it to Evanston. If anybody in this Holiday Inn recognizes TransCoastal's uniform culottes, I've already had it. Now I'm getting desperate, Dwayne. I know enough about you to get you sent away forever, and since you got me into this, you're going to get me out."

Silence.

"Dwayne, if you think I'm kidding you, just keep watching the news. Because if you don't get me some money or get me out of here somehow, I'm going to start calling the newspapers and the TV stations, and your name will be the first thing that comes out of my mouth. I've never let on that I knew what was going on before because I was going to hit you up for some good money when I had enough to bargain for. Well, I'm letting you off easy. We can call all those past jobs even, but you've got to come through now."

There was another long pause. Then, "I don't know, Meaghan. You've got more to lose than I do if you do that."

"You think so? Keep watching the news, Dwayne." And she touched the phone with the receiver just for an instant.

"Wait!" he said. "Don't hang up. Meaghan?" Maxwell raised a triumphant fist toward Wally.

"Yes, Dwayne?" she said.

Defeated, Lindgren said, "Where are you?"

"Room six-eighteen. Evanston Holiday Inn."

"I'll find it. Meet you in the lobby in forty-five minutes."

"What's it going to be, Dwayne? Money or helping me get out of here?"

"I can't risk going anywhere with you, Meaghan. Your face has been plastered all over town on TV and probably in the papers already."

"Then forget about meeting me in the lobby. Come to the room and knock four times. And Dwayne, if it's going to be money, it had better be a lot."

He hung up without a reply.

Meaghan trembled. "I can't believe I did that," she said.

"Nor I," Maxwell said, shaking his head. "You almost made me wonder if Wally was right about you or not!"

"You think he'll show?" Margo asked.

"Absolutely. But he's not bringing help or money. He's got to get Meaghan out of the picture. If she hadn't seen him at the airport, *he'd* be turning *her* in to us. But now he knows she'd put him at the scene of the crime, and he can't risk that. He wants to make sure she's found silent in the morning."

"That's the part we didn't talk about," Meaghan said. "How are you going to be sure that doesn't happen?"

"Don't worry, dear," Maxwell said. "I think we have enough people here to protect you. We *want* Dwayne to show up with a weapon. But we *don't* want him to have it out in your presence. Here's how we want it to go . . ."

When Dwayne Lindgren got off the elevator on the sixth floor just less than fifty minutes later,

Cedric Maxwell's two agents were stationed at either end of the hall, just inside the doors that led to the stairwells.

The adjoining doors between rooms 618 and 620 were open, and Margo and I stood in the dark in 620, close enough to see and hear everything in 618 where Meaghan sat on the bed with her shoes off and Wally stood to the left of the door. Maxwell positioned himself on the other side of the door. Both had guns drawn.

We heard four quick knocks, and Meaghan jumped. Maxwell signaled her to take her time. She slowed and moved toward the door. She peered through the peep hole, backed up slightly and nodded. Maxwell nodded back.

She stepped close to the door and said shakily, "Dwayne?"

"Yeah, open up."

Meaghan turned the deadbolt lock and unlatched the chain lock, then ran into 620 as Maxwell reached over and opened the door. Dwayne Lindgren took one step into the room with his hand inside his coat and felt the cold steel of Wally's .38 calibre snub-nose press against his cheekbone.

Maxwell's pistol was jammed against his temple on the other side. "On your face!" Maxwell said. "Flat, right now!" When Lindgren was on his belly on the floor, Wally yanked his hands up behind him and handcuffed him, pocketing the killer's automatic pistol. Lindgren swore in a whimper as Maxwell's men came in from the hall, guns trained on his head as Maxwell searched him. He found a .22 clipped to Lindgren's leg, just above the ankle.

"If you were worth the hunk of lead, I'd blow you away right now," Maxwell said.

Meaghan turned to Margo and fell into her arms. "He wouldn't really do that, would he?" she said.

Meaghan was Meaghan to the very end.

Moody Press, a ministry of the Moody Bible Institute, is designed for education, evangelization, and edification. If we may assist you in knowing more about Christ and the Christian life, please write us without obligation: Moody Press, c/o MLM, Chicago, Illinois 60610.